P9-BJD-409

The solid front door was closed. Jase went forward and laid his hand on the brass handle, but didn't open it immediately, instead surveying her with an assessing gaze.

Samantha took a determined step toward the door. He'd have to open it or move out of the way.

Instead he lifted his other hand and closed it about the nape of her neck, pulling her to him. Then as her mouth parted in startled protest he leaned toward her and she felt his warm lips on hers, a slight pressure parting them farther.

DAPHNE CLAIR lives in subtropical New Zealand with her Dutch-born husband. They have five children. At eight years old she embarked on her first novel, about taming a tiger. This epic never reached a publisher, but metamorphosed male tigers still prowl the pages of her romances, of which she has written more than forty for Harlequin Books, and more than sixty all told. Her other writing includes nonfiction, poetry and short stories, and she has won literary prizes in New Zealand and America.

Readers are invited to visit Daphne Clair's Web site at www.daphneclair.com.

TAKEN BY THE PIRATE TYCOON
DAPHNE CLAIR

~ RUTHLESS TYCOONS ~

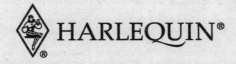

HARLEQUIN®

TORONTO • NEW YORK • LONDON
AMSTERDAM • PARIS • SYDNEY • HAMBURG
STOCKHOLM • ATHENS • TOKYO • MILAN • MADRID
PRAGUE • WARSAW • BUDAPEST • AUCKLAND

If you purchased this book without a cover you should be aware that this book is stolen property. It was reported as "unsold and destroyed" to the publisher, and neither the author nor the publisher has received any payment for this "stripped book."

Recycling programs for this product may not exist in your area.

ISBN-13: 978-0-373-52763-2

TAKEN BY THE PIRATE TYCOON

First North American Publication 2010.

Copyright © 2009 by Daphne Clair.

All rights reserved. Except for use in any review, the reproduction or utilization of this work in whole or in part in any form by any electronic, mechanical or other means, now known or hereafter invented, including xerography, photocopying and recording, or in any information storage or retrieval system, is forbidden without the written permission of the publisher, Harlequin Enterprises Limited, 225 Duncan Mill Road, Don Mills, Ontario, Canada M3B 3K9.

This is a work of fiction. Names, characters, places and incidents are either the product of the author's imagination or are used fictitiously, and any resemblance to actual persons, living or dead, business establishments, events or locales is entirely coincidental.

This edition published by arrangement with Harlequin Books S.A.

For questions and comments about the quality of this book please contact us at Customer_eCare@Harlequin.ca.

® and TM are trademarks of the publisher. Trademarks indicated with ® are registered in the United States Patent and Trademark Office, the Canadian Trade Marks Office and in other countries.

www.eHarlequin.com

Printed in U.S.A.

TAKEN BY THE
PIRATE TYCOON

CHAPTER ONE

IT WAS Auckland's society wedding of the year. Although the bride had come from nowhere, the daughter of a former employee of Sir Malcolm and Lady Donovan, the groom was the Donovans' only son—and until today one of New Zealand's most eligible bachelors.

Following the ceremony in the historic missionary church at Donovan's Falls, Sir Malcolm's widow had organised a lavish reception at Rivermeadows, the family's gracious nineteenth-century homestead.

Samantha Magnussen had dressed for the occasion in a superbly designed rich-cream silk summer suit. Her naturally blonde hair was styled to a shining cap that swung forward at her earlobes. A hot-pink wide-brimmed hat trimmed with huge gauze roses shaded her face from the sun and reflected a subtle warmth to her complexion. The slim purse she carried and the elegant Italian-made shoes on her narrow feet perfectly matched the colour of the hat.

Samantha had never been able to acquire a suntan, but the expertly sprayed salon version gave her bare arms and legs a convincing golden glow.

She might find the light blue eyes she'd inherited from her

Scandinavian forebears colourless and uninteresting, the refusal of her hair to thicken or take any kind of curl frustrating, and certainly her mouth lacked the lush fullness that many women would endure the pain of injections to achieve. But Samantha knew she was fortunate in having regular features and smooth, fine skin. With skilful application of the right makeup her nondescript looks could pass for a kind of beauty.

And today she wanted to look her best.

Approaching the bridal couple where they stood at the top of the wide steps leading to the long veranda and the homestead's massive front door, she stifled a stab of jealousy as Bryn Donovan bent his handsome dark head to his bride and smiled at her with an intimacy that Samantha had never experienced. Not with Bryn, not with any man.

He was still talking to the last person to shake his hand when his new wife raised her brown eyes to Samantha.

Noting the difference in height between herself and Bryn's bride, she asked herself with a touch of cynicism why tall men seldom chose women close to their own stature.

There was only one way to get through the next several hours—slip into her Society Event persona. Pinning on her well-practised social smile, she introduced herself to Rachel, and as Bryn turned at the sound of her voice, added, "Bryn's a very good friend." Reminding herself: *And that's all.*

She put a hand on his shoulder and kissed him, a brief, nonsexual peck on his warm but unresponsive lips, surely allowable on his special day. Some people routinely greeted close friends this way.

Then she stepped back, her hand involuntarily sliding down the front of his jacket before returning to her side.

"Congratulations, darling," she said lightly, making Bryn's

brows lift a fraction, his smile turn quizzical. "I never thought you'd do it. I guess even the tallest tree in the forest has to fall sometime." *But not in my direction.* Her smile, hiding piercing disappointment, didn't waver.

Bryn laughed, easily. "Very philosophical." He hooked an arm about Rachel's waist and pulled her closer. "I'm a lucky man."

Samantha had seen other intelligent and good-looking— and wealthy—men snared by women with little to offer beyond a pretty face and a passable pedigree. Still, although Rachel might lack the pedigree, apparently she wasn't short of brains—a historian and author, no less.

Studying the young woman for a moment, Samantha saw wariness in the dark eyes, perhaps uncertainty, but also determination in the tilt of her chin. Maybe Bryn had met his match. "You know," she told him, with reluctant respect for his choice, "I'm sure you're right. Does she know what she's taking on?" Bryn could be a formidable presence.

"I do," Rachel answered firmly. "I've known Bryn since I was five."

So keep off the grass? Samantha couldn't help but be intrigued. Even with Bryn's ring newly on her finger Rachel Donovan wasn't convinced of her husband's love.

Squashing a temptation to whisper in the bride's ear, *Don't be such a goose! He's all yours now, so make the most of it!* Samantha said with genuine sincerity, despite the pang it cost her, "Well, I wish you all the best. I hope you'll both be very happy." She certainly wanted it for Bryn. Her gaze shifted to him, but already Rachel had recaptured his attention—the man couldn't keep his eyes off her for a minute.

Samantha turned to walk away, her mouth unconsciously

curving again in a wry, self-mocking smile, her eyes clashing with a deeply green, brown-flecked masculine stare no more than a metre or so away, that startled her with its glittering suspicion and animosity.

The eye contact lasted only long enough for a fleeting impression of a hostile storm-sea glare under lowered brows, a strong nose with flared nostrils, a clear-cut upper lip and a fuller, sensuous lower one, and a couple of weeks of dark growth lightly framing a wide, stubborn and very masculine chin.

The designer-stubble, just-got-out-of-bed look had never appealed to Samantha, yet despite his smouldering glare the beard shadow seemed to emphasise instead of detract from the man's striking good looks.

She moved through the crowd on the spacious lawn, skirting chattering groups of guests holding champagne flutes or coffee cups.

Glad she'd had the forethought not to wear stiletto heels that would have sunk into the ground and impeded her progress, she paused only to take a full glass from one of the circulating waiters before coming to a stop under the shade of a huge old magnolia, and realised she was almost panting, as if she'd been running across the short-cropped grass instead of walking at a perfectly normal pace.

She'd not even looked round to see whom she should be making small-talk with. It might be a private occasion, but many business decisions had their genesis in chance—or not-so-chance—meetings at gatherings like this. There were movers and shakers here, potentially important contacts.

None of them impinged on her consciousness, her inner eye still focused on the stranger who had stared at her with such inexplicable ferocity.

His hair had been a shoulder-length mane of unruly dark brown, shot with streaks that glinted golden-red in the sun. She'd have assumed he'd had it professionally highlighted, except that the luxuriant, uneven waves looked as if they'd been trimmed with hedge clippers and pushed back from his forehead with impatient fingers. Like the other men here he was dressed formally, yet despite the pearl-grey suit of impeccable cut and fit, a snowy-white shirt and olive-green silk tie, he seemed totally out of place.

The tree cast a broad, protective shadow over chairs set about small tables holding plates of gourmet hors d'oeuvres. A quick glance at the guests seated there showed her no one she knew, and right now she felt unsettled, not up to making polite conversation with strangers.

Perhaps she should have brought along a partner—any of a number of male friends would have been happy to oblige. But she hadn't wanted the bother of maintaining at close quarters a pretence of enjoying herself, and making sure a companion actually did.

Anyway, she didn't need a crutch, or a smokescreen. No one would imagine that Samantha Magnussen was without an escort for any reason but her own choice.

Taking a few steps out of the shade, she paused to admire the Donovan mansion. Beautifully maintained, it had stood the test of time with its white-painted timbers and long windows, gabled roofline and tall chimneys.

She was the daughter of a man who had made a fortune erecting much-admired public buildings and some very exclusive private homes. Throughout her childhood the family had moved from one show house to another, each bigger and more opulent than the last, superb advertisements for her father's burgeoning business.

Yet she had a special liking for beautifully crafted old houses like this one, with its air of permanence and grace, home to successive generations of one family.

She had been curious to see Rivermeadows for herself. That her first chance to do so had been Bryn Donovan's wedding invitation was perhaps ironic.

He and his bride were posing for photographs now on the wide steps, along with their attendants and various family members, the groups shifting from one take to the next.

The man who had fixed his inimical glare on Samantha mounted the steps with others for several shots, and Samantha wondered where he fitted in.

For a second time his eyes found hers. Even at this distance she felt the full force of his hostility, as if something had thumped her in the chest.

What was *with* the man? She was certain she'd never seen him before in her life. He surely had no reason to dislike her at first sight.

Even this late in the afternoon, perspiration was forming on her forehead under the brim of her hat. Looking away from the group on the steps, she caught sight of a path leading to the rear of the house. It would be cooler there, and the guests had been given carte blanche to enjoy the gardens for an hour while the wedding party was photographed, before a formal meal.

Slowly she made her way to the rear of the house where people gathered on a shaded terrace. Past the swimming pool, an archway invited a stroll under tall trees with flowers and plants beneath them. No one seemed to be taking up the opportunity and Samantha was alone as, sipping at her champagne, she followed the winding path until she found a small summerhouse shrouded in flowering climbers.

Removing her hat, she stepped into the dim, shady interior and sat down on a narrow bench. Then she leaned her head against the latticed wall and closed her eyes, allowing the peace and privacy to quiet her confused emotions.

She hadn't expected to feel so despondent about Bryn Donovan's marriage. It wasn't as though he'd ever shown the slightest sexual interest in her, even before Rachel Moore returned from working overseas and apparently bowled him over. For as long as Samantha had known him Bryn had been involved with some other woman, any hiatus between female companions soon filled.

For the past three years he and Samantha had been business associates, becoming firm friends. She wasn't sure when she'd begun to hope that friendship might one day morph into something more. And now it was too late.

Since the announcement of his engagement she'd tried to banish fruitless might-have-beens, persistent fantasies of how it would feel to be loved by a man like him.

Almost thirty years old and in good health, in charge of the very successful firm she'd inherited from her father, Samantha had the respect of the commercial community, the loyalty of a select circle of friends, and her choice of several undemanding and pleasant men whenever she needed one at her side for social reasons, or simply felt like enjoying male company.

Everything she needed or wanted was hers, and yet...

Something alerted her—perhaps a shadow falling across the doorway, a soft sound, or a change in the air around her.

Reluctantly opening her eyes, she recognised with a start

the looming masculine bulk that blocked the entrance. He'd un-knotted the green tie that matched his eyes, and it hung loose, the collar of his shirt unbuttoned and showing a vee of sun-browned skin. He was watching her, unsmiling, leaning on the doorframe with arms crossed, one black-leather-shod foot angled across the other ankle.

A pirate, she thought fancifully. Or a brigand. With his raffish beard-growth and untameable hair he seemed not to belong in the twenty-first century.

She sat up straighter, the movement sending her hat sailing silently from its perch on her knee to the leaf-strewn floor of the summerhouse. "Are you following me?" she demanded.

Someone had told her once that she had a smoky note in her voice, although apart from a brief teenage fling with cigarettes she'd always been a non-smoker. For some reason, at this moment the slight huskiness was more marked than usual, and she wished she could start over, make the question sharp and clear.

It didn't appear to have impressed this man. The way a corner of his mouth twisted was almost a sneer. "Are you running from me?" he countered.

"Of course not. I don't even know you. Do I?" She supposed it was possible they'd met somewhere before—*a long time ago in a land far away?* Mentally she shook herself. The champagne must have gone to her head. She should have eaten some of the delicious-looking finger foods being offered.

The man answered, "You don't know me." His voice was velvet underlaid with gravel, dark and full of unspoken, sinful promise. He straightened, then swooped forward to pick up the hat that lay between them, holding it in his left hand as he introduced himself. "Jase Moore. Brother of the bride."

Samantha put down the empty champagne flute and stood, wanting to leave but she'd have had to step round him. Well-inculcated good manners made her offer her hand. "I'm Sa—"

"I know." Jase Moore didn't crush her bones as some men did, but his clasp was strong. "Samantha Magnussen, a *very good friend* of Bryn's."

She had always used a firm grip, but her fingers when his closed around them seemed about to melt. Releasing her, he said, "I wouldn't be the first man to follow you."

How could she answer that remark? From someone else it might have been an attempt at flirtation, but this man's blunt-force manner seemed to preclude anything as light and inconsequential as flirting.

A shiver ran through her, for no reason except that Jase Moore, although no longer touching her, was standing so close she could hear the quiet sound of his breathing, see the amazing length of his thick black lashes. The unfathomable green of his eyes looked darker here in the leafy shadows, the pupils enlarged. He was taller than she'd thought, his eye level higher than hers.

She stepped back, her legs coming up against the seat behind her. "Why did you?" she asked. "Follow me? It wasn't because…" *because you like me.* All too obviously he didn't. Although she still couldn't figure out why his dislike seemed to have such force, let alone why it had been so instant.

Realising it would sound like part of some playground tiff, she didn't finish the sentence.

He did it for her. "…because of the usual reason?" A sort of smile flashed briefly, more like a half-snarl. "No." He was blocking her way out of the small space that held them, his head tilted to one side while he inspected her. "Whatever your relationship might have been in the past with Bryn, it's over now. He's married to my sister, and that makes him off-limits to you or any other woman."

Samantha's cheeks burned. Humiliation and shock fed a searing, swift anger. "You don't know what you're talking about!" she said, but her voice shook and she knew she sounded less than convincing, appalled that he'd read her so easily and quickly.

"*You* do," he argued. "So watch your step, lady."

Her head lifting, she steadied herself, regaining a semblance of her normal detached composure, and said precisely, "Whatever might or might not have been between Bryn and me is none of your business." Damned if she was going to explain herself to this arrogant jerk. "And if you don't trust your new brother-in-law, you'd better take it up with him."

"I don't see him carrying a torch," Jase Moore replied with infuriating calm. "All the heat was coming from you. The ice princess look is only skin deep. Interesting."

Inwardly Samantha was quivering, feeling exposed, naked. How could this stranger have divined in seconds her most private, well-protected secrets, without even exchanging a word or a touch? But she wouldn't crumble under the assault.

She directed her chilliest stare into his watchful, probing eyes. Strong men had wilted under that look. "Either you're drunk and delusional," she said, "or you have an overactive imagination. You know nothing about me, and I certainly have no desire to know anything more about you. That you're a boor and a bully is unfortunate for your sister, but we don't choose our relatives. For the first time I'm grateful I don't have brothers. Now, may I have my hat, please? I'd like to go back to the party."

Something sparked in the dark eyes that maintained their steady regard, and for a moment she thought he wasn't going to comply. Then a grim smile touched his mouth and he gave a small nod, as if acknowledging an adversary. He stepped aside and held out the hat to her, allowing her to reclaim it.

She restrained herself from crushing the brim in her fingers as she brushed by him and walked away without hurry, resisting the urge to flee in haste, and annoyed that her legs felt shaky.

The nape of her neck prickled. She would *not* look back to see if Jase Moore was watching her retreat.

A boor and a bully, huh? Jase grinned with sardonic appreciation as Samantha Magnussen, her back straight and shining blonde head held high, rounded a bend in the path that took her out of sight.

Water off a duck's back, lady. He'd been called worse, though never in such frigidly polite tones. And if the ice princess knew what was good for her, she'd take heed of his warning.

Rachel wouldn't have thanked him for acting the big brother on her behalf—if she ever found out she'd tear strips off him. But the lifelong habit of looking out for his fiercely independent little sister hadn't been obliterated by her years away from her family, nor by her decision to marry Bryn Donovan. The uncertainty in her eyes when Samantha Magnussen kissed Bryn and called him *darling* in that come-hither voice of hers had set all Jase's protective instincts into overdrive.

And they hadn't been appeased in the least by the woman's enigmatic remark about never thinking Bryn would get married, or the measuring glance she'd given Rachel, as if sizing up a rival. After that kiss, which to Jase's sharpened eye had seemed to last a fraction of a second too long, she'd trailed her hand down Bryn's body in an almost proprietary gesture. Or perhaps she just hadn't been able to keep herself from touching him.

Bryn had seemed oblivious, at least on the surface, to the fleeting but unmistakable regret on the blonde's perfect oval of a face, and he'd have missed the Mona Lisa smile with which she'd turned from the happy couple.

It was the smile that had made Jase pursue her once the photographers had finished with the family. A smile like that could mean anything—and if it meant she wasn't yet finished with Bryn Donovan, that she had hopes of enticing him away from Rachel, someone had to set her straight.

CHAPTER TWO

THE formal part of the reception over, evening drew in and Samantha meant to quietly leave, and approached Bryn's mother to thank her and say good-night.

"But you must stay for the dancing!" Lady Pearl insisted. A small, pretty woman, she had a knack of getting her way without seeming at all pushy. The big front room and adjoining formal dining room had been cleared, with a three-piece band set up in a corner, and once the newlyweds had circled the floor it quickly became crowded. "There are some nice young men without partners," she said. "I'll introduce you."

Before Samantha could make a graceful excuse her hostess had laid one light but determined hand on her arm and lifted the other to signal someone. "Let me take your purse. I'll put it on the hall table for you. Did you leave your lovely hat there?"

Samantha had, along with her jacket, revealing a sleeveless matching separate bodice held by thin beaded straps, the beading continuing around the low neckline and repeated at the hem just below her waist. A woman in a plain black dress relieving guests of surplus jackets and accessories had hung the hat and jacket on a brass coat-stand for her.

Reluctantly she allowed Lady Pearl to take her purse, not realising which *nice young man* had responded to their hostess's summons until she felt an instantly recognisable male presence at her side.

"Jase," the older woman said, "is Rachel's brother. And Jase, this is—"

"We've met," he told her.

"Oh, good! You know each other." Apparently oblivious to the abruptness of his interruption, and Samantha's frozen expression, Lady Pearl benignly ordered, "Well, then, get out there and enjoy yourselves."

She stood expectantly beaming, and after a moment Jase lifted his brows and held out a hand that Samantha finally took, allowing him to lead her into the crowd.

"You don't have to do this," she muttered as he turned her to face him. "It wasn't my idea."

"Didn't think it was." His free hand settled on her waist and he brought the other, enclosing hers, close to his chest. "I'm doing it for Pearl."

So was she, not wanting to appear rude. Somewhat to her surprise he led her into a smooth ballroom step rather than the more energetic dancing favoured by the younger guests. Automatically she leaned against his guiding hand as he took her into a smooth turn, his thigh brushing hers, and the slight contact awoke a peculiar sensation deep within her.

As if he'd felt it too, his eyes met hers, then he blinked fantastically long, thick lashes and turned his gaze over her shoulder.

Samantha swallowed, and said, simply for something to fill the silence between them and banish the odd intimacy of that moment, "Where did you learn to dance?"

He shrugged. "My mother, when I was about to attend my

first high-school ball. She said the girls would be dressed up and looking their prettiest, and if I was going to step all over their toes it would spoil their evening."

"I'm sure the girls appreciated it." She kept her tone light and a little dry. They'd probably appreciated his appearance too. Even in his schooldays he must have had female class-mates a-flutter.

She herself had always preferred men to be clean-shaven with neatly groomed hair. Yet on this particular man the unkempt look seemed entirely natural and somehow added to his…charm was hardly the word. To whatever it was that had made all her senses annoyingly spring to full-alert when he'd taken her hand and swept her onto the floor. A reaction so rare that it alarmed her.

He'd discarded the jacket and tie altogether now. In white shirt and grey trousers he looked relaxed, his movements assured and imbued with masculine grace.

"And," he was saying, a glint of humour—mixed with something else—in the eyes again meeting hers, "it was a pretty neat way to get a girl into my arms."

It was the something else—the suppressed but unmistak-able spark of masculine awareness that made her realise she wasn't the only one finding their forced proximity unsettling.

Rachel and Bryn danced by them. Rachel was smiling up at her new husband, and he bent to fleetingly kiss her lips, then said something to her as he drew back.

Rachel laughed, shaking her head.

And Jase's hand hardened on Samantha's waist, bringing her closer as he said in her ear, "Don't even think about it. About him."

Her head snapped backward and she glared into the hard

olive-green gaze, no trace left of humour. "I wasn't thinking about anything, except how soon I can decently get away."

"From me?"

"That too," she said frostily, an annoying heat in her cheeks as it occurred to her that if she said any more he'd assume she wanted to leave so she could nurse her supposedly broken heart.

Which, she assured herself, wasn't broken or even chipped. Maybe a tiny bit cracked, but that would heal. She said, "I'm not fond of crowds."

One dark brow twitched upward, and something new came into his eyes. Something she hoped wasn't pity. Quickly she added, "It's hot in here." An excuse for the guilty, girlish flush.

Jase nodded curtly, and before she could guess his intention he'd steered her through open French doors, propelling her to the back terrace.

A group of smokers indulging their habit were the only people there. At an unoccupied table for two Jase pulled out a chair and said to Samantha, "Sit. I'll get you a cold drink. What do you want?"

"I don't need a drink." Then it occurred to her that the offer was an excuse. He could leave and not come back. A way out for them both from their hostess's misguided pairing. "I'll be fine, if you—" *leave me here* was on the tip of her tongue, but unexpectedly he shrugged and dropped into the chair opposite hers.

"Okay," he said. "Probably a wise decision."

"I'm in no danger of getting drunk," she said, more sharply than she'd intended.

"You've had at least four glasses of wine, and haven't eaten much. Is that how you keep that figure?" He ran a quick, critical glance over her, the expression in his eyes veiled when they returned to hers. "Dieting doesn't do you any good, you know."

He'd been watching her? "I don't diet," she snapped, then deliberately moderated her voice. "And four glasses in four hours won't take me over the limit." Her last two drinks had been apple juice. She never overindulged in alcohol, but had learned to hold her own with business contacts who did, often making one glass last while they downed several.

"You're driving?" Jase frowned.

"We're a long way from the city," she pointed out. Central Auckland was a good hour away from the rural community of Donovan's Falls.

"You can afford to hire a driver, surely?"

Samantha wondered if he'd been asking questions about her, of the Donovans or their guests. Or had simply recognised her name. "I prefer to drive myself," she said shortly. "Do you work in construction?" Surely she wasn't so well-known that many people outside the field would have connected her with the firm that still bore her father's name, and the wealth he'd accumulated.

"Nope. Well, you could say that now, I guess. Bryn just hired me. Is a timber merchant in the construction business?"

Had he been unemployed? "They can't do without each other," she said. "That was good of Bryn." Presumably he'd offered the job for Rachel's sake.

Something flickered across Jase's face and was gone. Then he said, "He's going to be quite a useful brother-in-law."

Behind the careless tone she detected a hint of something suspiciously like mockery, reflected in his darkened eyes by the soft light from carriage lamps affixed to the wall of the house.

Even if he didn't share his sister's brains or ambition,

maybe he'd had some kind of job, and Bryn had offered a better one. In any case, unemployment was no disgrace, though many people were embarrassed to admit to it.

She doubted this man shared that emotion. He was blunt to a fault himself. "What did you do before?" she asked.

He grinned as though for some reason the question amused him. "Mainly messed about with computers in my parents' garage."

A geek? That might account for his lack of social niceties.

"And helped out on their farm now and then," he added.

A man and woman emerged from the house holding glasses of wine. Seeing Jase, they changed direction and walked towards the table. "Hey there!" The man grinned down at them. "Are we interrupting something?"

"No," Samantha said before Jase could answer. "Actually I was just about to leave." She made to get up but the man looked dismayed and laid a large, work-roughened hand on her shoulder to stay her. "Don't move for us," he urged. "If it's a private conversation—"

Jase said, "If it was, you'd have just shoved your big manure-covered gumboot so far into it there'd be no hope of continuing anyway. Samantha Magnussen, this is my brother, Ben. And April, who for some unknown reason actually married this big dumb lug."

Ben aimed a swipe in the general direction of his brother's ear, expertly dodged by Jase, and then hooked a couple of chairs from an empty table for himself and his wife. After seeing April seated he said, "Nice to meet you, Sam," and settled his sizeable frame into the other chair.

His grin was engaging, his gaze curious but friendly. Samantha didn't even mind him shortening her name at first acquaintance. Despite his close-shaven cheeks and short-back-and-sides and the tie he still wore, he reminded her of a big, harmless Labrador. There was some family resemblance to Jase in his eyes and hair colouring, but there it ended.

His wife was dainty and shy and in the conversation that followed Samantha learned that April was from the Philippines, and they had met when Ben holidayed there a year or so earlier. Anyone could see they adored each other.

She felt a stab of envy. It seemed to be her day for it.

Because this was a wedding celebration? Perhaps it had something to do with her thirtieth birthday looming. But many of her contemporaries hadn't married until well into their thirties, or weren't going to bother at all, even if they had a partner. It was nothing to be concerned about.

In fact she'd never seriously thought about marriage, even when she'd begun thinking about Bryn in...*that way*. It had been just something that might happen at some vague future time.

When a pause came in the conversation April turned to Samantha. "A nice wedding," she said in her prettily accented voice. "Rachel looks very beautiful."

"Yes, she does." Samantha tried to inject enthusiasm into the conventional agreement, avoiding Jase's eyes.

"She's a lovely girl," April added. "Very nice."

Samantha prepared herself to listen to a litany of Rachel's virtues, but the other woman merely said, "I'm sure Bryn will be a wonderful husband."

I'm sure too. Samantha didn't say it aloud.

Ben said to his brother, "I hear you're going to work for our new in-law. Bit of a change from your flippin' games, staring at a ruddy screen all day. Ruin your eyes," he warned.

"Beats staring at the back end of cow and getting covered in sh—ah—dung."

"Huh!" Ben grunted. "About time you got yourself a proper job, you effing layabout." He glanced at April as though she might object to the euphemism, but she merely shook her head reprovingly, trying to hide a smile.

"Okay, so I'm not a horny-handed farmer like you," Jase said, and gave his brother a mock salute. "Backbone of the country and all that."

"Gonna drive a truck for Bryn?" Ben inquired, grinning. "Stack timber? Do some real work for a change?"

Samantha couldn't read the glance Jase threw her before answering. "Probably a bit of driving, for a start."

As the brotherly banter continued, April turned to Samantha. "Take no notice of them. They're always like this. Just because Jase didn't want to be a farmer, and Ben can't imagine doing anything else. But they're very fond of each other really."

Jase was lazily grinning at his brother's teasing, a grin quite different from the guarded teeth-flashes he'd directed at her.

Samantha forced a smile. An only child herself, when young she had watched the sometimes rough-and-tumble interaction of her friends and their siblings with wistful envy. And here she was again, the outsider, the one who didn't belong.

Attacked by a wave of melancholy, she stirred and stood up. "I really have to go," she said, directing her social smile at Ben and April. "It was nice meeting you."

To her surprise Jase rose too. Coming to her side, he touched her arm, saying, "You're sure you're okay to drive? I can take you home."

They were entering the house and she said, astonished,

"Why would you do that? Anyway, you must have been drinking too."

"One glass of bubbly to toast the happy couple," he replied. "Pearl asked for volunteers to stay cold sober and see that everyone got home safely."

A consummate hostess, Pearl Donovan had thought of everything.

"I'm fine," Samantha assured him. When they reached the wide, empty hallway she walked in a rigidly straight line down the centre of the carpet runner to the long hall table and retrieved her things. Stiltedly she said, "Thanks for the offer."

The solid front door was closed. Jase went forward and laid his hand on the brass handle but didn't open it immediately, instead surveying her with an assessing gaze.

Samantha took a determined step towards the door. He'd have to open it or move out of the way.

Instead he lifted his other hand and closed it about the nape of her neck, pulling her to him. Then as her mouth parted in startled protest he leaned towards her and she felt his warm lips on hers, a slight pressure parting them further.

Before she had even gathered her wits enough to push him away he released her.

Outrage at his daring to kiss her, and shock at the unexpected, contradictory sensations he'd aroused held her speechless. Her instinct was to slap his face, but with her hat in one hand and her bag in the other that wasn't a real option. "What the *hell*—" she started to say, and stopped as she heard her voice shake.

"You don't taste of alcohol," Jase Moore told her calmly. He opened the door and stood waiting for her to pass through. "I guess you'll be all right."

Not trusting her voice, she lifted her head and gave him a stare that would have frozen the fires of hell, then swept by him without a word.

Ignorant, sexist opportunist! The man should be dressed in a bearskin and dragging a wooden club.

She negotiated the steps and followed the lights along the driveway to the temporary parking area in a close-shorn paddock. A security guard at the gate nodded to her and added the powerful beam of his torch to the lights set around the perimeter, until she located her car.

The guard waved to her and she drove slowly out of the gateway and accelerated along the road, tempted to put her foot down and express her anger by recklessly breaking the speed limit. She settled instead for calling Jase Moore every insulting name in her vocabulary, under her breath.

Thank heaven, she told herself when she finally ran out of epithets, with luck she'd never see the man again. If he was working as a truck driver for Donovans she'd hardly be likely to run into him at their city premises, even though her firm did a great deal of business with Bryn's.

Why the hell—she asked herself the question she'd been unable to finish asking in the Donovans' hallway—why had he kissed her? He certainly didn't *like* her.

Had he meant to humiliate, show her she was vulnerable to male physical power? That he had the upper hand and she'd better heed his earlier warning?

And as for that *You don't taste of alcohol*, as though he were some kind of human breathalyser...

Automatically dimming the headlights as another car crested a rise and sped towards her, she gave a tiny, scornful laugh.

She remembered the feel of his mouth on hers, the tang of

pine and another unnameable, somehow seductive scent in her nostrils. The strength of his fingers curling about her nape.

And she remembered too, that when he drew back and released her, within the curve of the light beard his cheeks had showed a subtle colour along the bones.

Something stirred inside her. A peculiar mixture of fierce satisfaction and an unwanted but not unpleasant thrill replacing mortified fury.

He'd kissed her because he'd wanted to. Because he couldn't help himself. And then he'd had to excuse it somehow. Because...

Samantha bit her lip. No use denying, ignoring it. Because despite his suspicion, his antagonism, and her own justifiably furious reaction, despite the hostility that arced between them like an alternating electrical current, something else sizzled under the surface. Something primordial, elemental.

Something sexual.

When Jase rejoined his brother and sister-in-law, holding a glass of amber liquid, Ben gave him a quizzical look. "Moving in high-flown circles now, eh, mate? She doesn't seem your type."

"She isn't," Jase answered shortly. "Bryn's mother set us up."

April asked, "Is that why she was uncomfortable?"

Jase looked at her in surprise. "I suppose." He hadn't thought anyone else would have noticed. He and Samantha had been unwillingly thrown together but good manners prevailed.

He'd expected Samantha would dance like a mannequin from a store window, looking great but stiff and haughty. Instead she'd been fluid and warm, supple and sinuous, easily following the slightest pressure of his hand, her steps matching, even anticipating his every movement.

For a moment or two he'd found himself wondering if she'd respond like that in bed, what it would be like to make love to her.

Not that he was likely to ever find out. Nor really want to, he assured himself.

Ben said, "She's a looker." Then grinned. "Too classy for the likes of you."

"Uh-huh," Jase grunted and picked up his glass to drink. The taste didn't erase the memory of Samantha Magnussen's soft lips, the warmth and sweetness of her mouth—so at odds with her aloof manner. Even the kiss—an impulse he should never have given in to—had only had the effect of making her amazing, almost translucent blue eyes turn glacial.

"Hey, that went down fast." His brother broke in on Jase's thoughts. Ben's brows curved upward. He'd gathered his own and his wife's empty glasses and pushed back his chair. "I thought you weren't drinking."

"Ginger ale," Jase replied, and declined Ben's offer to get him another.

"Do you like her?" April inquired quietly as her husband disappeared inside the house.

"Hardly know her," Jase said. "We had one dance, she was feeling hot so I brought her out here."

She certainly doesn't like me.

Hardly surprising. She'd wanted to hit him after he'd kissed her. He had seen the reflexive movement of her arm before she dropped the hand holding that absurd hat to her side. He'd almost hoped she would, that at last she'd show some loss of her unwavering control.

Like what he had glimpsed when she greeted Bryn, a moment of real human emotion behind the lightly spoken words with their ambiguous undercurrent. But there was nothing ambiguous about the brief but telling betrayal of her feelings. She hadn't been a happy guest at the wedding.

After the confrontation in the summerhouse he'd watched her from a distance, seen her greet several people, exchanging hugs with some of the women, one of whom did so with a piercing, "Samantha, *darling!* I haven't seen you in an age!" From some of the men she'd accepted a kiss on the cheek, but never offered her lips. Once she laid a hand on a man's arm for a second or two, making some laughing remark. The man—sixty-ish, grey-haired but still good-looking—smiled at her with unconcealed admiration and said something in return at which she laughed again.

The ice princess could turn on the charm when she wanted to. But when the man leaned closer she moved almost imperceptibly back, though keeping her smile intact. Not the way it had been with Bryn, as if she couldn't stop herself touching him.

Showing a capacity for pain and passion under the Nordic cool. The woman was a walking contradiction.

Should he care? His only concern was for his sister. He wouldn't allow anyone to hurt Rachel.

CHAPTER THREE

SAMANTHA was unable to put the disturbing, infuriating Jase Moore out of her mind. For weeks, then months, she'd scarcely seen Bryn. She let her managers deal with him when business made contact necessary, and kept away from gatherings he might be expected to attend—with his wife at his side. Her social life was reduced to close friends and inescapable obligations, giving herself time to get over the surprisingly deep hurt of losing a man she'd had no claim on in the first place.

It couldn't be that hard to return to viewing him as a friend and business colleague whose company she enjoyed. And her circumspection had nothing to do with Jase Moore and his misguided attempt to frighten her off.

It wasn't as if Bryn had ever appeared to notice her perhaps too-tentative attempts to signal her growing interest—the lingering handshakes, the sincerity and warmth of her smile, the occasional fleeting touch. Now she wondered, if a perfect stranger could pick it up at first glance, had Bryn known all along? Known and not given her any encouragement because he simply didn't find her sexually attractive? The thought made her inwardly squirm. Another reason to avoid him for a time.

She immersed herself in carrying on her father's business,

his life's work. A brilliant builder, he had employed the very best workers, even poaching them without conscience from other firms, but had remained staunchly attached to traditional practices. He had never learned to use a computer himself, although conceding the need for them and paying his Information Technology Manager a handsome salary.

Samantha felt it was important to keep up-to-date if her firm was to maintain its premier position in a crowded industry. She booked for a one-day seminar on Future-Proofing Your Business, the star attraction being an American speaker whose books about the changing face of management she'd admired.

After seeing his name she hadn't bothered to read the rest of the programme, sure the steep fee would be worth it just to hear him.

His keynote speech, first on the programme, convinced her she'd been right, but she was puzzled when before the next session she saw none other than Jase Moore carry a laptop computer onto the stage.

Her first thought was, *It can't be.* Her second that he was there as a technician. Maybe he'd left Donovan's already or been shifted from the transport department to one more to his liking.

He placed the computer on a table beside the microphone and lifted the lid. His white shirt, worn with dark trousers, was open at the collar, the sleeves rolled to the elbow. Obama casual, and it suited him.

Then the chairwoman stepped forward and began to introduce him. Samantha looked down at the programme in her hand, passing over a glowing CV of the guest speaker to the next page. Among a list of names and subjects, she saw "The Future of the Interfaced Workplace." Speaker: J.S. Moore.

"Mr Moore," the chairwoman was saying, "began his

career in computer games, hitting the jackpot before he was out of his teens with his popular pirate series, 'Pinnaces, Pillage and Plunder,' and 'Hunters of the High Seas.'"

Samantha's mouth fell open and she quickly shut it again. She'd never played computer games, nor even looked at those included with her office programme, but she had seen TV ads touting the virtual environment games, and no one could miss the ubiquitous posters, T-shirts and novelty items emblazoned with the titles and characters.

"At the same time," the chairwoman continued, "he was experimenting on his father's farm, marrying farm machinery and electronics, leading to designing revolutionary systems for the agricultural sector, which are now used worldwide."

The woman glanced at the notes in her hand. "Recently he's been developing systems and machinery for industrial use, with a particular interest in safety and the use of virtual reality simulations for training, and the integration of office and workface into a seamless digital environment."

Jase's deep, confident voice woke Samantha from a whirling daze. She dimly recalled glancing through a couple of news articles mentioning the ubiquitous pirate games and their spin-off merchandise, and being somewhat surprised that their creator was apparently a multi-millionaire, fast catching up to the top ten richest people in the country.

His name hadn't stuck. And she had no interest in agricultural machinery, so that too had passed her by.

Helped by computer-generated images on a large screen behind him, Jase clearly and fluently described a future of machinery and even surgical instruments controlled by operators simply thinking their commands to specialty computers.

Already Samantha used computer programmes to show

clients three-dimensional "plans" for buildings, but he promised "a real-time physical walk-through of virtual buildings," then went on to describe more ground-breaking work in fields that once were the domain of science-fiction.

When he was done, in answer to a query he quoted statistics about production losses due to industrial accidents, and called on Bryn, whom Samantha hadn't seen seated in the front row, to come to the microphone and describe how Jase had improved production and safety at Donovan's Timber.

At morning tea, among the throng around the tables bearing scones and muffins to go with their tea and coffee, Bryn caught her eye and made his way to her with Jase in tow.

Bryn kissed her cheek and said, "Haven't seen you for a long while. What did you think of my brother-in-law?" He put a hand on the other man's shoulder. "You met Jase at my wedding, didn't you?"

Samantha gave Jase a nod of recognition. "Your presentation was very interesting." She wouldn't give him the satisfaction of expressing surprise that he was not the idle loser he'd allowed her to imagine.

His "Thanks" was preceded by a faint twist at the corner of his mouth, as though he knew she found the compliment difficult, and that amused him.

Bryn said, "Some of the systems he put in place for us would probably work for you. In fact if we used the same programmes it could cut time and effort—even expense—for both our companies."

Samantha just stopped herself from physically recoiling. Jase must have noticed. The curl at the corner of his mouth grew, and the hint of a dimple creased his cheek. She said, "I'll think about it."

A tubby man in a brown suit joined them, loudly quizzing Bryn about his experience with Jase's services.

Jase moved closer to Samantha's side and said sotto voce, under the chatter all around them, "Glad you took my advice."

Something prickled along her spine. "I don't remember you giving me *advice*."

"Bryn hasn't seen you for a while?" He nodded as if in approval, making her hackles rise further.

She clipped out, "We're both busy people."

Casting her a penetrating glance, he said, "How are you doing?"

Tempted to retort, *What do you care?* or preferably, *Get lost!* Samantha said shortly, "Fine, thank you. And Rachel?" she inquired pleasantly, trying to be civil as well as deflect the conversation from herself.

His eyes narrowed for an instant, becoming even greener, then he said evenly, "Happy. And I mean her to stay that way."

"Surely that's up to Bryn?" Samantha's eyes went to his brother-in-law, still in conversation with the other businessman. "And Rachel. Who's a grown woman," she reminded him. From her own brief encounter with Rachel, the woman was no wilting flower. She'd seemed entirely capable of protecting her own marriage.

"She's still my sister," Jase said. "Getting married doesn't change that. And I warn you, if necessary I'll play dirty."

She cast him a glance that would have refrozen the melting icecaps of the Antarctic, hiding a shocking flash of temper that made her palm itch to slap his head from his shoulders.

She wasn't answerable to him for her feelings, or his misconceptions. "You're the only one playing games," she said. "They don't interest me."

Bryn turned to confirm something with Jase, and as the conversation continued between the three men she thought of slipping away, but hesitated, not wanting to appear to be running from Jase.

Then the other man reclaimed Bryn's attention, and it was too late. Following on from their discussion, she asked dryly, "How much *driving* did you do before you were allowed to play with Donovan's computers?"

For a moment he looked blank, before apparently recalling the conversation with his brother at the wedding reception. Then he laughed. "Quite a bit—travelling round the country to all the branches so I'd know how they operated and what was needed. Bryn wanted me to start with his sawmills, designing systems to increase safety."

"That sounds like him," she said, recalling Bryn's almost haggard face after a near-fatal accident in one of Donovan's mills when a worker in a careless moment forgot to observe its stringent safety rules. Her gaze strayed to him, still listening patiently to the man in the brown suit.

Jase's brows drew together. Before he could say any more the crowd about them parted and someone touched Jase's arm. A pretty brunette with bright lipstick on her mouth, she wore a black suit over a white blouse.

"Mr Moore," she gushed, "that was a wonderful presentation. I'd love to have you come and talk to my executive staff."

Samantha edged aside, and the man who had been monopolising Bryn turned his attention to the newcomer.

Bryn smiled at Samantha and said, "How about we get out of this scrum and find a place where we can catch up while we finish our coffee?"

Still riled at Jase, she let Bryn lead her to an empty lounge bar where the counter was closed. He sat at a small table across from her, and relaxed into the tub chair.

He was one of the few people with whom she felt safe lowering her guard. Taking over Magnussen's after her father's death hadn't been easy. Bryn too had become head of a family business on his father's death, and their similar experiences had given them a unique bond. Unlike her, he had spent years within the family firm before it became his, yet instead of taking advantage of her lack of experience, as some shrewd operators had, he'd offered advice and support.

And she wouldn't kowtow to his brother-in-law's erroneous view of her, give up a friendship she valued, simply because Jase Moore didn't believe she could control her feelings.

Ironic, considering she'd spent a lifetime learning to do just that.

Twenty minutes went by quickly, and she slipped into the familiar territory of stress-free friendship, with only a slight lingering discontent that she'd missed her chance of something deeper.

At her last board meeting one of the members had resigned due to illness. Not so long ago Bryn would have been at the top of her shortlist for a suggested replacement, but she'd not put his name forward, afraid her feelings for him would be reactivated. Now she made a decision and put the invitation to him, firmly dismissing a twinge of trepidation. If Jase found out…

When they returned, the area outside the hall was nearly deserted, a few people hastily finishing their coffee or tea, and Jase lingered near the double door, one half already closed. Samantha saw the sharp look he directed at her and his brother-in-law, and instinct made her move closer to Bryn, her shoulder brushing his arm.

Jase's eyes narrowed dangerously as Bryn put a light hand on Samantha's waist to usher her into the big room before him.

They slipped into seats at the rear, Jase next to Bryn at the end of the row. As Samantha put her bag out of the way under her seat and straightened up she saw him fold his arms and stretch out his long legs.

For the rest of the seminar he was never far away each time she looked around her. She avoided him at lunch by sitting with a couple of other women, swapping war stories about sexism in business, but later, as she seated herself at the closing dinner, Jase slid into the chair beside her.

Apart from a cool nod of greeting she tried to ignore him, concentrating on the food and the other diners around the table. But she was conscious of his hands picking up his knife and fork, his voice when he spoke to others at the table, his laugh when someone cracked a joke, his leg brushing against hers as he reached for one of the bottles of wine on the table.

"Samantha?" He poised the bottle over her glass.

"Thank you." She nodded without looking at him, and watched as with a steady hand he poured ruby-red wine into her glass before refilling his own.

He replaced the bottle and said in a low voice, "Where did you and Bryn get to during the tea break this morning?"

Her stomach clenched, remembering the look he'd directed at her on their return. He didn't have the right to interrogate her, and she wasn't going to be intimidated. "Somewhere private and quiet," she said, driven by an obscure urge to needle him, because he certainly had no compunction about provoking her.

"Why?" Jase's hand curled around the stem of his glass but he didn't lift it.

"To talk," she said. "Privately and quietly." She turned to stare into his eyes, daring him to inquire further.

She might have known it would have no effect. He said, "What about?"

A knot of resentment had lodged in her chest. "If you really need to know," she drawled, keeping her own voice down, "we made plans to run away together and set up house somewhere and have wild, uninhibited sex for days on end."

The flash of shock and anger in Jase's eyes, the sharp breath he drew gave her a moment of fierce satisfaction. Then she recalled his renewed warning earlier—*If necessary I'll play dirty*—and a shiver slithered down her spine.

His eyes ominously glinting, Jase said flatly, "Not funny."

"It wasn't really meant to be. And what else isn't funny is the way you've been stalking me all day."

"Stalking?"

"Yes. Give it a rest, will you? It's beginning to get on my nerves."

"I didn't think you'd be so easily rattled, ice lady." His eyes had turned speculative, curious. "What are you hiding beneath that touch-me-not cool of yours?"

Her heart gave a heavy thud as though she'd just been confronted by a physical threat. "I'm not sure what you mean," she said coolly. "What do you hide behind that fuzz on your face?"

He laughed. "Laziness, I guess. Can't be bothered shaving every day. You don't like it?"

"It's nothing to do with me," she told him. Any more than her friendship with Bryn was anything to do with Jase.

She ought to lay his suspicions to rest instead of goading him. But by making excuses she'd be tacitly admitting she was in the wrong. Besides, there was a certain pleasure in unsettling Jase Moore, a secret revenge for his low opinion of her.

He'd been right when he said the ice was only skin deep. Again today he'd made her angry—and frightened. She didn't want him—anyone—to know how thin and fragile her protective coating was. That underneath the composed and confident business leader with a reputation as a gutsy and unflinching negotiator was a flesh-and-blood woman who hurt like anyone else.

But who didn't dare show it. Jase Moore was one of the very few people who had seen through the brittle surface she presented to the world, and the only one who had done so without her permitting it.

That was why he made her so nervous.

Jase drove through the night to his home, an hour or so away near the provincial city of Hamilton, his mind annoyingly fixed on Samantha Magnussen. No woman had got under his skin the way she did.

Kissing her after the wedding had been a mistake. Irritated by the distant contempt with which she'd met his warning, he'd wanted to shake her chilly control. And figured that was a surefire way to do it.

Or so he'd tried to explain it to himself. After the fact.

At the time he'd simply done what seemed a damn good idea—for five seconds. And then justified it with that implausible comment about not tasting alcohol.

What he'd tasted had been unexpectedly warm, soft lips, feminine and sweet, that left him wanting more. The memory was still amazingly vivid.

Seeing her today, he'd wanted to do it again. At the same time, when she looked at Bryn and spoke of him with a note of affection in that sexy voice of hers, he'd wanted to shake her.

The small, mysterious smile on her lips when she'd turned away from the other man on his wedding day had set off warning bells in Jase's head, and then she'd looked straight into his eyes, her poised, cool beauty concealing hidden fires. That kind of understated allure could drive any man wild.

It hadn't escaped him that despite his warnings she'd made no promises not to try seducing Bryn, made no assurance that she had given up hope.

An old school friend of Samantha's had organised a fundraiser for the Red Cross. "A kind of upmarket market," she'd told Samantha enthusiastically. "A fun night for bargain hunters, with live music and a bar—to get the punters in the mood for spending," she added, with a shrewd grin.

The big room was filled with Auckland's art lovers, tycoons and socialites sipping champagne, peering at the donated goods and simply chatting—or in many cases networking.

Samantha had donated one of her father's investment paintings to the cause, and dressed for the occasion in a plain black sheath with subtle silver threads in the weave. A fine silver chain around her neck held a single black pearl.

She saw Bryn, his wife by his side, an arm about her waist while they talked with another couple. Rachel wore an amber satin dress, and her thick dark curls were swathed atop her head in a way that Samantha's pale, straight hair would never achieve.

Of course it was inevitable that someday—or night—she and Rachel would be in the same place at the same time. The only real surprise was that it hadn't happened sooner.

While she hesitated about approaching the couple, Jase

appeared from behind them, holding between his hands three wineglasses, two of which he adroitly passed to his sister and her husband.

Then, as if he'd felt Samantha's gaze, he shifted his stance and his eyes found her despite the crush of people between them.

Someone touched her arm, and she turned gratefully to greet an older couple she'd known since childhood. They'd been among the first to arrive offering sympathy and help after her mother's death, and had made an effort to console the bewildered and stricken thirteen-year-old. Although hardly able to respond to their kindness at the time, she'd kept in touch with them ever since.

They drifted off after obtaining a promise from her to visit in the near future, and she found Jase at her elbow. Although many of the men were in black ties, he was tieless, a crisp white shirt open at the neck under an out-of-fashion unbuttoned waistcoat.

He still favoured the unshaven look, but the dark shadow on his chin had never been allowed to develop into a full beard. She suspected his style, if it could be called that, owed more to an uncaring attitude than deliberation, yet his dressed-down appearance amounted to a sort of dishevelled chic that few men could have carried off.

His eyes held hers with the intensity of a high-end laser. "Samantha." His gaze dropped over her low-cut, clinging black dress before his eyes returned to her face. The glitter that had appeared in the darkened depths evoked contradictory emotions in her—wariness mixed with disconcerting pleasure because he couldn't hide the fact that, unwillingly or not, he found her attractive.

He said, "You look…very glamorous."

"Thank you." She realised she was holding her glass in a death grip, and loosened it, giving him her accomplished social smile. "What are you doing here?"

"Supporting a good cause. Like you, I guess. Bryn's here too with Rachel."

He was watching her closely—she supposed looking for a reaction. Keeping her expression serene, her voice neutral, she said, "Yes, I saw them."

It wasn't the first time since she'd stopped avoiding him that she had run into Bryn. They went on as if nothing had changed. She even listened with only a small hitch in her heartbeat when he mentioned Rachel, although the note in his voice might have made a lesser woman weep with envy.

Jase still held her eyes, and to her surprise quiet laughter escaped from his throat. "You're something else, ice lady." There was a note almost of unwilling respect in the enigmatic remark.

Samantha was on the brink of a retort when the subject of their discussion entered her field of vision behind Jase, and she hastily closed her mouth.

Then Bryn was there, his lips brushing her cheek as he greeted her, and Rachel said, "Nice to see you again, Samantha."

They exchanged chitchat, and then moved as a group to compare opinions on the wares being offered. Rachel looked beautiful but was there a tiny shadow in her brown eyes, and behind the wide smile? An expert in putting on a good face herself, Samantha recognised one when she saw it.

Jostled by punters eager to inspect the goods, somehow Samantha and Jase got separated from the other two, and she found herself standing next to him while he examined a carved jade abacus with a hefty price tag.

"That's beautiful," she said involuntarily, admiring the intricate patterns on the beads. "I suppose it's worth the asking price." Which was rather steep.

"It is to me," he answered, then put down the abacus and pulled out a credit card to hand to the person behind the table.

For someone in the forefront of an almost unimaginable technological future, it seemed an odd choice. Curiosity getting the better of her, she said, "What will you do with it?" She didn't suppose he was going to use it for his calculations, when he had his pick of state-of-the-art computers.

"Enjoy it," he said. "And admire it, as a fine example of early computing."

"Oh? I never thought of an abacus as a primitive computer." And she hadn't thought of him as a sentimental collector.

"Not so primitive. An example of true genius. Whoever invented the abacus way back sometime BC, when he first spun his beads in a row he was setting us on the road to the computerised society."

"Or she," Samantha suggested.

He inclined his head. "Or she," he agreed, picking up his purchase and nodding thanks to the cashier. "Are you an ardent feminist?"

"I suppose. *Ardent* may be pushing it a bit."

"I guess," he murmured, even as she continued,

"I'm no banner-waving activist."

He said, "No, you just get on with doing it rather than shouting about it, don't you?"

"I'm not knocking those who do the shouting," she told him. "We need them—people passionate enough to fight and suffer for what they believe in." She picked up a silver Georgian coffeepot, smoothed a hand over its elegant shape and put it down again.

"What are you passionate about, ice lady?" Jase asked. He sounded genuinely curious, and a voice inside her whispered caution.

She shrugged. "My company, my father's legacy."

Making to move on again, she found him blocking her with the immovability of a stone statue. "That's all?" he queried.

"Isn't it enough?"

"You had your own business in Australia, didn't you?"

"A small one." She wondered where he got his information, although it was no secret. "We specialised in renovations, with an emphasis on sustainability and energy saving." Things her father had dismissed as "airy-fairy greenie-babble."

"And you left it to come back and run your father's company." He sounded almost disapproving.

"Of course," she said, oddly angry. "I always knew it would be mine one day. My inheritance."

He looked as though he wanted to say more, but then he nodded, and shifted so she could step by him.

Jase let her move away, but his eyes followed her for minutes afterwards. He knew she was aware of his concentrated gaze. It was in the set of her head, the tension in her bare, smooth shoulders. Not looking back, she took cursory interest in several things before leaving the tables without buying any of them.

She'd greeted Bryn tonight showing none of the unguarded emotion Jase had seen the first time he'd laid eyes on her. But he hadn't missed the uncharacteristic warmth of her smile, nor the searching look she directed at Rachel, fleetingly revealing something strangely like sympathy.

That thought brought his brows together and his mouth into an obdurate line as he watched Samantha greet someone else with what he'd come to think of as her company face—the serene, synthetic smile, not reaching the topaz-blue eyes with their enigmatic gaze.

What was going on behind that beautiful, frustratingly emotionless facade? Why would she be *sorry* for Rachel? Surely that spelled trouble.

His sister might seem to be a mature, successful woman— hell, she *was*. But there was a touching innocence about her all the same. He suspected she'd been so busy with her studies and career for the past ten years that she'd let personal relationships—male/female relationships anyway—pass her by. And she'd had a crush on Bryn Donovan since she was barely fifteen, something her whole family knew but had never mentioned to her.

Jase was pretty sure that when the family moved away from Rivermeadows after Rachel's last year at high school, his mother had been relieved. Not that she wouldn't have trusted Bryn, but a pretty girl with her heart in her adoring big brown eyes must be a temptation to any red-blooded young man. Jase and his brother had found it rather hilarious that Bryn seemed to be the only one at Rivermeadows who hadn't noticed how she felt about him.

So when she'd come back into his life, it was nice that Bryn had fallen for her too. Or—uneasily Jase considered the possibility—maybe had been flattered into marrying her, because Rachel had never been that good at hiding her emotions.

Not like Samantha.

During Bryn's first Magnussen's board meeting Samantha gave a summary of the seminar they'd attended, skipping over Jase's contribution as lightly as possible.

But when she'd finished, Bryn strongly suggested that Magnussen's could benefit from Jase's expertise. It wasn't, she thought ruefully, what she'd been looking for when inviting him to join the board. After he'd finished singing Jase's praises, he said, "I should tell you that Jase Moore is my brother-in-law, but I know from experience that he's very good at what he does. I'd like to move that Magnussen's ask him to do a preliminary survey of its systems company-wide."

The murmurs of interest left Samantha no choice but to put the idea to the vote, with a foregone conclusion.

This was business and—following in her father's giant footsteps—she'd always put business first. Although she kept her hands firmly on the reins, unlike him she gave respectful weight to other opinions before making decisions. If she vetoed the idea the board members would wonder why.

When she phoned, after she'd given him a brief outline of her reason for calling, Jase said, "I gather Bryn's been talking me up to you." His voice was level, and perhaps she was imagining the hint of censure in it.

"As a member of my board. They want you to have look at our systems."

The silence that followed had an edge to it. She wondered if he was going to turn her down. Finally he broke the pause. "How long has he been on your board?"

Her breath hitched. So Jase hadn't known that. "Not long. Are you interested?" she demanded. "In doing business with Magnussen's?"

He was going to turn her down, she was sure. But after another sharp pause he said shortly, "Next week I have some time. You can show me round and I'll do an assessment."

CHAPTER FOUR

SAMANTHA asked her IT manager to take Jase around the office building and discuss its computer systems, but when it came to the construction side she usually took site visitors around herself—clients, investors, inspectors. An excuse to get down to where the heart of the company really was.

Site bosses were often less than keen to have outsiders blundering about a half-finished building, asking questions and getting in the way. Her presence smoothed their path. There were safety concerns too and hers was the ultimate responsibility for anyone on site as well as her own workers.

Wearing overalls, earmuffs and hard hats, she and Jase followed the site manager over uneven ground, wet and slippery with recent rain, scattered with odd bits of timber and metal and piles of other materials. The day was cool with a biting wind, grey clouds above the city threatening rain. A torn piece of paper scooted across the ground, lifting and falling.

The sounds of hammering were drowned by the roar of machinery and the steady thud of a pile driver. The building was to be the Auckland headquarters of an international insurance company, its foundations driven deep into the earth.

Samantha inhaled the smell of new wood, which always made her tingle with pleasure. She saw Jase glance at her and give a small, slightly surprised smile.

Yes, she wanted to tell him, *this is what I'm passionate about.* She just didn't get down often enough to where the actual work took place.

Wasn't he passionate about his work? He had surely made his millions doing something he obviously loved. So where did he get off criticising her dedication to her company?

And it was safer to be angry at his arrogance in presuming to know so much about her, than to admit the pull of his arresting good looks and raw male appeal.

Overhead a crane swung a solid iron reinforcing bar through the air, and lowered it delicately to where yellow-helmeted men stood waiting to fit it into place.

Jase shouted questions to the site manager, making occasional notes in a handheld computer device and sometimes taking photos with it. He went round the entire site and asked more questions of some of the workmen, and occasionally of Samantha herself.

When they returned to the site office Samantha removed her earmuffs and hard hat and shook out her hair. After shedding her boots and overalls, she took a comb from her bag and quickly used it.

Jase watched her with interest. Her lipstick had faded, the cold wind had brought colour into her cheeks, and the tip of her nose was pink. Her feet were bare—she hadn't yet put on her shoes—and he had a fleeting vision of what she might have been like as a child. "Was your childhood happy?" he asked her, suddenly wanting to know.

"What?" The comb in her raised hand, she paused to stare

at him. The pose reminded him of a Greek statue. A thin sweater showed the outline of her breasts, and close-fitting jeans hugged her hips and legs. "My *childhood*?" she queried, dropping her hand.

"You did have one, didn't you?"

She gave him a withering look. "Why do you want to know?"

Good question. And one he wasn't prepared to answer. "Bryn said your mother died when you were young."

For a moment Samantha felt betrayed. But it was common knowledge. The fact had even been included in a magazine article about her a year after she took over the company. "I was thirteen," she said.

"It must have been tough."

Her mother, though considerably younger than her father, had been killed by a brain aneurism, without warning. A shock for everyone. Samantha picked up her bag. "I've had a long time to get over it." But in fact she hadn't, had simply learned to live with the painful hole left in her life.

"Your father never married again?" She was on her way to the door, but he beat her to it, opening it for her and following her outside.

"No," she said as they walked to her car. "I'll give him that."

"What do you mean by that?" he asked.

Samantha pressed the button on her key ring to unlock the car as they approached. Jase stepped forward to open the driver's door for her.

"Nothing." She regretted the comment. "He was a good father. He did a lot for me." He'd always been happy to give her anything she expressed a desire for. As for those things that were inexpressible, that she'd not been able to articulate, no one could be expected to read minds, or irrational emotions. Certainly not a remorselessly practical man like Colin Magnussen.

She slipped into her seat, still thinking of her father and their complex, difficult relationship.

He *had* loved her, even though she'd been a disappointment to him, and perhaps he'd loved his wife more than she'd ever known. Certainly he'd never saddled Samantha with a step-mother. If there had been other women in his life, she'd never seen any sign of them when she was home for weekends and holidays from the exclusive boarding school he'd sent her to a few months after losing his wife.

After Samantha left home at twenty-one, removing herself from his overpowering shadow, and crossed the Tasman to Australia, she'd fully expected he would marry again. He wasn't too old to find another trophy wife—nor to father the son he really wanted.

But he hadn't. He'd simply become even more obsessively devoted to his business. And then he'd died.

Not wanting to think about that, she shook her head, and as Jase joined her in the car he asked, "Something wrong?"

Only my life.

Where had that come from? Her life was satisfactory in every way. She said, "Just thinking. Do you want to see another site?" As she spoke, rain spattered on the windscreen, quickly turning to a steady downpour.

"That's enough for today," Jase said, looking out at the rain. "This looks like it's going on for a while, and I've a few ideas to work with now." He glanced at his watch. "I'm hungry. What are you doing about lunch? Can we talk about this—" he lifted his electronic notebook "—while we eat?"

She took him to a restaurant close to the Magnussen

Building, where she often entertained business visitors and was well-known to the staff, and they were seated promptly at her favourite table. The background music was not too loud, so they could talk without having to raise their voices. After they'd ordered, Samantha went to the ladies' room and repaired her makeup.

Over her mixed seafood dish and Jase's ham on a kumara mash, they discussed his preliminary findings. For a time she almost forgot the latent bone of contention between them.

His smile, his quick brain and ability to think outside the square, the timbre of his voice, the subtle male scent that reached her when he leaned forward with his mini-computer to demonstrate on the small screen what he was talking about— all combined to keep her captivated. They sparked ideas off each other in a way she found unexpectedly stimulating.

Finally Jase put away his notes and they ordered coffee.

Stirring sugar into his cup, he said, "When I've seen all I need to understand your processes, I'll work on costings for you."

"Bryn said some of what you installed for him might work for us."

She felt his sharp glance, but he only nodded, saying in a neutral voice, "No point re-inventing the wheel. If it's out there anywhere in the world I'll find it. If not, I'll design what you need and get it built."

"At a price?" she murmured, and sipped at her coffee.

He shrugged. "You don't get me cheap." He leaned back a little, a hint of devilment entering his eyes. "But I've had no complaints so far." He looked all male and devastatingly sexy. Her reaction was predictable, and irksome, but she hid it, putting her coffee cup carefully back in its saucer.

He probably couldn't help himself. He had an innate

response to…well, to any half-decent-looking female, she assumed. Some men were like that.

There were film stars, singers, sportsmen, who had the same power to draw women effortlessly into their orbit. Partly as a result of fame and good looks, but there was something else, some indefinable quality that gave them an edge over other men.

Whatever it was, Jase Moore had it in spades.

He said, studying her with a slightly barbed meditative look, "Did you ask Bryn onto your board just to spite me?"

Samantha raised her brows, coolly derisive. "I asked him because he was the obvious candidate." Her hand curled about her cup.

"So you did what's best for your business." His voice was dry.

"And I trust him…as a good friend."

His eyes searched her face, the expression in them seemingly made up of part anger, part suspicion and possibly— making her instantly defensive—part concern. "A friend. And you're okay with that?"

"Of course," she answered curtly.

He was still regarding her with that disconcertingly perceptive stare. Finally he said in a flat tone, "Then you were never really in love with him."

"I never said I was," she answered, her voice very even and only slightly acerbic. "That was your…fantasy."

"Uh-huh." Disbelief coloured his voice, lurked in his eyes. He still didn't buy her disclaimer. "Speaking of fantasies…"

He stopped there and looked down, closing his hand about the coffee cup. Samantha said, "What?"

Jase raised his head. "You don't want to know."

But the renewed gleam in his eyes, the wry smile on his

mouth, gave her a clue. For a moment their eyes held, and a peculiar feeling invaded her midriff.

The man had no right to indulge in fantasies about her.

She reminded herself, picking up her cup and sipping at it, that while he might have a physical reaction to her appearance, it didn't mean he liked her as a person. She put down the cup and returned a carefully dispassionate gaze, her tone intentionally mocking. "*That* lurid?"

He laughed. "Not lurid at all," he said. "Surprisingly... innocent. I saw a little girl, pale and pretty and not quite sure of herself. Lonely, maybe. Wistful. Longing for...something. Something she was afraid she'd never have, but was more important to her than anything."

Samantha felt her mouth dry, and her cheeks grow cold.

Her tongue slipped over her lips, but the moisture only lasted a second. Drawing a deep breath, she tried to steady the whirling in her head. He'd been right when he said she didn't want to hear this. How could he know more about her than she did herself? In the Middle Ages he'd have been burned at the stake. "That's..." Her voice cracked and she tried again. "That's quite an imagination you have."

A strange expression flitted across his face. He picked up his cup and drained it.

Samantha swallowed, trying to ensure her voice had returned to normal. "I'm ready to go."

He nodded, not commenting on her still almost full cup. Then he studied her for a second. "Are you okay?"

She raised her brows. "Of course."

When she took out her credit card he protested, but gave in when she said he was a guest of Magnussen's and that of course it would go on the company account.

Outside, the downpour had abated a little, but the lowering clouds had turned black and the light was dim, ozone sharpening the air.

Standing under the canopy outside the restaurant, Samantha turned to Jase. "Are you coming back to the office?"

He shook his head. "I'd like to get to my computer while this morning's still clear in my mind. Thanks for lunch. And the site tour." He paused, his eyes searching her face. "You're sure you're all right?"

"I only have a few steps to go." Deliberately misunderstanding him.

He nodded, a twist of his mouth acknowledging that. "I'll be in touch." Unexpectedly he bent his head and brushed his lips across her cheek before turning towards where he'd parked his car.

Ten minutes later, sitting at her desk staring into space, she could still feel the touch of his mouth.

Her secretary entered, and stopped before she reached the desk. "Are you all right?" she asked. Just as Jase had.

Samantha snapped herself out of a confused reverie. "Yes. What is it, Judy?"

For the rest of the day she firmly kept Jase and his unsettling remarks at the very back of her mind.

When she reached home that night after working late, she was tired but restless. Following a quick meal of tinned soup and a couple of pieces of toast, she poured herself a glass of wine and switched on the TV but found nothing she wanted to watch. Then she flicked through the daily paper before flinging it aside and picking up a book that also failed to hold her attention.

She put it down on the elegant metal-and-misted-glass coffee table, smoothed the cushion she'd been resting against, deciding she needed softer ones, and began aimlessly wandering about the spacious apartment.

She'd bought it after selling the last house her father had built for his family, less than a year before her mother's death. It had seemed full of life when her mother was alive—she was always hostessing parties or business dinners, celebrating birthdays, anniversaries, holidays, having guests to stay. Following her death it had seemed empty, too large for Samantha and her father, and it was certainly far too big for Samantha alone, even if she'd kept their housekeeper on.

Here she had a cleaner who came three times a week and left everything spick and span. There was nothing for her to do.

Maybe she should get a cat. Or a dog. Only the regulations in her building didn't allow either. Some of the residents kept birds, but she'd always had a feeling of angry empathy with caged birds, even knowing that those bred to it wouldn't survive in the outside world.

Her thoughts kept circling around Jase and the extraordinary so-called fantasy he'd regaled her with.

She shivered. *No one* knew how she'd felt as a little girl. He'd been guessing.

Every only child must have felt lonely at times. And didn't all children long for something—a puppy, a bicycle, a special doll, a baby brother…or their parents' attention?

Jase hadn't said anything specific and unique to her.

Had he deliberately played with her mind, like a phoney stage clairvoyant speaking in generalisations and knowing gullible members of the audience would refer it to themselves and unwittingly give clues to further the illusion? A stirring of anger grew into a cold rage. Stupid of her to have fallen for that cheap trick. And what had he thought to gain from it?

At least, she hoped, she hadn't allowed him to see how much it had affected her. She wasn't a child any more, but a grown woman who had learned how to hide her feelings, to appear impregnable, in absolute control of herself and her surroundings. Of her emotions. Proving to her father that when it came her turn to run the firm he'd worked so hard and long to build, that he'd poured his whole life into, she wouldn't let him down. That his little girl, as he'd used to call her, was as tough and strong and indomitable as himself.

A second glass of wine, breaking her usual limit when home alone, didn't help her inner turmoil, only made her inexplicably want to cry. Of course she didn't give in to the maudlin impulse. She hadn't cried since her mother's death and she wasn't going to start now.

Working with Jase wasn't as difficult as she'd feared, though she was always conscious of tension between them, the undercurrent of sexuality that was never totally absent. Determinedly businesslike, she was pleasant but impersonal, and he seemed willing to go along with that, though occasionally she caught a slightly acerbic gleam in his eye, an unsettling curl to his mouth when he looked at her, his eyes resting on her for a fraction longer than necessary.

They visited another Magnussen's site, a private home for a wealthy Chinese family who had particular requests for curves and pillars that signified good fortune. Samantha actually had a secret preference for building homes where people would live, families grow up, though she wouldn't admit to Jase that she didn't always love the concrete-steel-and-glass structures that formed a large part of her firm's business.

Eventually she gave him a name tag and carte blanche to

visit any of the company's operations after clearing it with the site managers. When he'd collected the information he wanted, he didn't contact her until he had finished a preliminary report.

Together they pored over diagrams, pricings and plans spread over drafting tables in her office. He'd e-mailed them to her computer, but this way she found it easier to comprehend them. Rigidly she suppressed her inevitable interior response to his smile, the accidental brush of her arm against his sleeve, the brief waft of his personal scent when he reached across to point something out to her.

At times a comment of his or a question of hers led them into other areas than the immediate task at hand.

She made a passing remark one day about wishing they could go back in time and visit famous buildings that had succumbed to disaster or decay over the centuries. And Jase said quite casually, "Mmm-hmm. Some of the world's best physicists believe that time travel will be achieved some time in the present century."

"Seriously?" Samantha queried. She straightened from the chart in front of them to stare at him.

"Seriously," he confirmed. "It seems that scientifically it's not impossible."

It had to do with black holes in space and other concepts she'd never really understood, but the way Jase explained the basics led her to exclaim, "You should have been a teacher."

"You think? *My* teachers would turn in those early graves they claimed I was driving them to."

"But you must have been bright!"

"If I was, it didn't show. I think I spent more time in detention than in class."

She regarded him thoughtfully. "I suppose you were a rebel."

Shrugging, he said, "A pain in the posterior. Barely scraped through my final exams. My parents despaired." Momentarily he looked regretful. "I try to make it up to them. Eventually I got a degree in computer science and physics."

"Didn't anybody recognise your potential?"

"A late bloomer," he said, then admitted, "I did get pretty good marks in maths at school. And science was okay, but I was banned from the lab after...well, a couple of unilateral experiments that were...um, less than successful."

Samantha tried to look disapproving, but couldn't help a laugh escaping.

His eyes lit with curiosity, he said, "I've never seen you do that before."

"Do what?" She stepped back from him, automatically checking for some gesture she'd made.

"Laugh so naturally. And *don't do that!*" he added, scowling.

She blinked. "Don't laugh?"

"No." He looked exasperated. "Don't close up every time I say something halfway personal."

Samantha stiffened. Then realised it was exactly what she'd done. Her face felt much as it did when her beautician applied a herbal mask that hardened over her entire face and would crack if she changed her expression.

Jase said, "You should laugh that way more often. It makes you look human."

Somehow that wounded her. "I *am* human!"

"Yeah," he said with a kind of scathing weariness. "And working hard at hiding it."

Her laugh this time was meant to be a scornful negation, but came out a shade too high and definitely not natural.

"That's a weird thing to say. As if you thought I was one of your computer-generated holographs or something."

"Uh-uh, not mine." Something new came into his eyes—something uncomfortably piercing, and he shook his head. "There are times, though, when I feel like Harrison Ford in *Blade Runner*."

In the film, Ford's lead character fell in love with a convincingly "human" robot, Samantha recalled. She'd seen it twice and had fought tears at the scene where Ford proved to the girl that her so-called memories of her family, her childhood, were false and she herself was a "replicant." Not a real person at all.

Making her voice crisp and damning, Samantha said, "You spend too much time with computers. Your imagination is running away with you."

"Maybe." But after a long, head-on-one-side, glinting look that engendered a defensiveness in her, he turned his attention back to the cost projection in front of them, apparently dismissing the unsettling exchange.

"I'll take it to the board," she promised some time later, "but we don't have unlimited cash to spend on expensive toys for boys."

Jase raised his dark brows.

"I know—I'm being sexist," she conceded. "But I've noticed how men's eyes light up at the idea of a new piece of machinery. Sometimes the cost is way out of proportion to the darn thing's usefulness. The more complicated it is, the more often it seems to break down. And once a sale's made, too many firms don't want to know."

"With me," he said, "you'll get an ironclad guarantee. Once I'm committed, I don't walk away."

* * *

Predictably, the board was impressed, and with only two diehards against, voted a budget for the proposal that Jase presented to them in person during their meeting.

After the others left, Jase said, "I'll send you a contract, Samantha, and you can have your lawyers go over it."

"Yes. Thank you." Her glance went to the photograph of Magnussen's founder that hung above the conference table, looking indomitable and maybe disapproving. Unconsciously she chewed at her lower lip.

"You have a problem?" Jase asked.

"My father might not have agreed with this."

"Your father's dead, isn't he?"

"Yes." She couldn't help a faint smile. No timeworn platitudes for Jase Moore. Not "passed on" or "gone." Simply dead.

"Did you always do what he wanted?"

"No, but he wasn't easy to challenge. He could never admit he might be wrong." And he'd been especially annoyed when his own daughter disagreed with him.

"What about your mother?"

Her mother had seemed to live to please her father. A former photographic model with a unique ability to shine in company, she'd been an asset in her husband's social and business life. Occasionally, with a winning smile and a light word or two, she'd poured delicately perfumed oil on waters he had ruffled, but always deferred to his opinions and his needs. The perfect mate for an autocratic man.

"She never argued," Samantha said simply. "Not that I remember. I suppose that's why they seemed to have a happy marriage."

All the same, Ginette Magnussen had not been without her own ways of softening her husband on occasion, using her femininity to advantage when nothing else worked. Something that came less naturally to Samantha. Aloud she said, "I guess I have too much of my father in me."

"You clashed?" Jase asked.

"More so after I left university and tried working for him. A mistake on both our parts."

"So starting your own business was a way to assert your independence and show him what you could do."

That perilously accurate insight startled her. "It's part of Magnussen's now," she said, "but operating independently. I try to implement some of its principles here, but the old guard are a bit suspicious of anything new."

"I've noticed," he murmured.

She sighed. "And I can't sack people who worked for my father for thirty years."

Jase flicked her a brief but intent glance, perhaps surprised, then his gaze shifted to the window. The temperature in the building wasn't uncomfortable, but outside high humidity mixing with heat made for a warm, muggy afternoon. A few wispy clouds hung motionless in the slivers of blue sky visible between the city buildings.

He said, "I could do with a cold beer and a long walk on the sand, with a cool breeze coming off the sea."

The image reminded Samantha she hadn't spent time at the beach for…so long she couldn't remember when she'd last felt sand between her toes.

He turned to her and must have seen something in her face. His strongly marked brows lifted. "You too?"

She gave a little shrug. "It's a nice thought." Her tone implying, *but of course you're not serious*.

"Why not?" he said as if making up his mind. "Are you ready?"

"Ready?" she returned blankly. "I didn't think you meant it."

"You said it was a nice idea," he reminded her.

"I can't afford to take off on a whim. Anyway, I need to work."

"Why? It's almost five o'clock." It was actually not yet four-thirty. "Will the business collapse without you in the next half-hour?"

She didn't bother to answer that, nor tell him she seldom left the office at five. "I just thought you'd want to be alone. Or at least, not with me."

His eyes gleamed derisively. "You need to do something about that inferiority complex of yours."

"What?" Samantha took a sharp inward breath. Then she saw the curve of his mouth and realised the remark had been gently sarcastic.

"You've got a mobile phone," he said. "If anything happens you'll get told."

A wayward urge to surrender to temptation struggled through her sense of responsibility. She tried to suppress it, but temptation won. So what if Jase had a knack of ruffling her feathers, if he didn't quite trust her? He was offering a stolen hour or so of peace and pleasure. It wouldn't hurt the business.

"If you mean it…" She still hesitated.

"I don't usually say things I don't mean." Something crossed his face. She wondered if he'd taken himself as well as her by surprise with the invitation. The gleam in his eyes intensified into something that aroused in her a treacherous awareness of his formidable masculine aura, fatally tempting. Softly, seductively, he said, "You know you want to do it, ice lady."

CHAPTER FIVE

His smile—wicked and knowing and dangerous—dared her.

Samantha imagined him with a cutlass in his hand and a bandanna tied about that unruly hair. Jase didn't look in the least like her mental picture of a man who sat before a computer all day. Perhaps he had a secret yen to command a pirate ship, and had let his fantasies run amok in the games he'd created.

"All right," she heard herself say, feeling as though she was agreeing to some risky voyage of discovery rather than a simple trip to the seaside. "I'll have to change."

She gathered the jeans and flat-heeled shoes that she kept in a small closet behind the door and excused herself before disappearing into her private bathroom.

In less than two minutes she emerged, collected her bag from the lower drawer in her desk, flicked her jacket off the hook behind the door and turned to him.

Her secretary looked up as they left. "I won't be in again today," Samantha said, ignoring Judy's astonishment. "You go home and I'll see you tomorrow."

"I'll drive," Jase said as they left the building, and he ushered her to a four-wheel-drive vehicle parked in the visitor's bay.

After leaving the car park he made a right turn, taking them away from the central business district and onto a motorway.

Samantha realised he wasn't heading for any of the popular inner harbour beaches within minutes of the city, nor across the Harbour Bridge to the North Shore. Instead they were travelling in the opposite direction. "Where are we going?" she demanded.

"To a beach," he said imperturbably.

She took her cell phone from her bag but as her finger hovered over the "on" button she found the idea of no one knowing where she was strangely liberating.

She lifted her finger and dropped the phone back in her bag again. "Where?" she asked again.

"The west coast," he said. "Not some tame, crowded strip of trucked-in sand."

The west-coast beaches—Piha, Muriwai, and their less-well-known neighbours—were wide and wild, a paradise for surfers but often dangerous. Lifeguard patrols routinely rescued swimmers swept out to sea by rips, board-riders who had over-estimated their skills, and fishers washed from the rocks by rogue waves. Of course he'd prefer one of those beaches.

Jase expertly negotiated a change of lane, swinging into a space between a bus and a red Volkswagen Golf, and later he took an exit off the motorway, stopping outside a tavern with a bistro and bottle store. "What do you fancy to drink on the beach? I could buy a bottle of wine. And some glasses."

It sounded too intimate, sitting on the beach drinking wine with Jase Moore. She wondered what she was doing here, why she'd rashly decided to join his spur-of-the-moment expedition. "I thought you wanted a beer."

"Do you drink it?" His surprise almost led her to lie and say yes. "Cider," she said, "would be nice. A small bottle, thanks."

"Wait here."

He came back minutes later with a six-pack of beer, her cider and a bag of potato wedges with sweet chilli sauce and sour cream. "Shouldn't drink on an empty stomach. Have some."

The sight and smell of the spiced wedges was too much to resist, and she reached for one, then another and another.

Rush hour traffic was heavy as they left the city but eventually the 4WD turned onto a winding road that showed glimpses of blue ocean between stands of white-feathered toe-toe, tough tiny-leaved manuka shrubs and tall, thick clumps of flax.

A few vehicles were parked on the gravel area at the end of the road, but the dun-coloured stretch of beach, streaked with broad bands of black iron-sand, looked deserted except for a lone surfer and a couple of distant figures with fishing rods on the flat-topped rocks at one end.

Jase parked beside a battered Holden station wagon with a roof-rack holding a surfboard. Samantha jumped to the ground and strolled to the sand. Jase took a rug from the back of his vehicle and joined her, and for a minute they stood inhaling the salty air and watching the breakers roll in, the blue-green water foaming on the crests and giving off a faint mist as they curled over and hurtled to the dark, glistening shore, a flattened, green-and-white mass of moving patterns leaving a long, slick tongue edged with creamy bubbles until the next wave came in.

"Tide's coming in, by the look of it," Jase said.

Samantha removed her shoes and they tramped over the dry, hillocky sand to a small hollow where he spread the rug and they sat down to sip at their cool drinks. They talked only desultorily, and Samantha began to feel pleasantly lazy and rather like a truant.

Jase crushed the empty single can he'd taken from the six-pack, and when she finished her cider he collected up the containers. Samantha shook out the rug and he stowed everything in their vehicle then said, "Let's walk."

They crossed the soft, still-hot sand to the smoother, harder part of the broad beach, where their feet made only shallow prints. Jase had discarded his shoes and rolled up his jeans, and Samantha swung her shoes in one hand. Just out of reach of the waves, they walked in silence for a while, enjoying the sea-scented wind that made Jase swipe hair from his eyes and teased Samantha's sleek style into unruly strands blowing every which way. The persistent roar and thump and hiss of the waves, and the shrill calls of gulls circling and swooping overhead made conversation unnecessary. The wind on Samantha's face felt like a blessing, and the damp sand soothed her feet.

She fell into a dreamlike state of uncomplicated bliss. There was nothing quite like a long, lonely shore for clearing the mind and replenishing the spirit.

Jase picked up a gnarled piece of driftwood and took a few steps towards the water, hurled the stick into a retreating wave laced with foamy white, then returned to Samantha's side.

The wind gusted briefly, raising gooseflesh on her arms so that she shivered and crossed them, rubbing the skin.

"Cold?" Jase said. "We can go back."

"Not really," she said. The gust had passed. "Let's go on to the end."

"Suits me."

There were masses of tiny black mussels clinging to the rocks, and she put on her shoes as Jase found a foothold and climbed, then turned and offered her his hand as she followed.

She hesitated before letting him pull her the rest of the way. His hand was strong and warm, and she stifled a rush of purely female appreciation at the ease with which he brought her up to his side.

They stood on a rock outcrop, where the waves beat against the far end, sending spray high in the air to splash down on the edge. Behind them loomed a rugged cliff edged with tenacious plants hanging over its lip, and at its foot a shallow cave held the blackened remains of a fire. Someone had barbecued their catch here perhaps, fresh from the sea.

Samantha picked her way over uneven rocks to a deep pool where small silver fish darted away from her shadow to disappear among seaweed and anemones, and crabs disguised in borrowed shells crawled across its sandy floor.

A bright blue starfish clung to the rock, and she squatted to inspect it. Then she spotted another, half hidden by gently waving seaweed.

Jase went on one knee beside her. "What are you looking at?"

She pointed, and he said, "Uh-huh. Pretty."

"When I was eight..."

She stopped there and Jase turned from admiring the starfish to look at her. "What?"

"Nothing. Just a memory from way back."

"Tell me," he said. It was almost a command, so compelling she very nearly capitulated. But caution prevailed.

She gave a light laugh and stood up, the backs of her knees stiff from crouching, and faced him again as he too rose. "You didn't bring me out here to bore you with stories of my childhood holidays." She'd had a sudden vivid memory of staying over part of the Christmas holidays with a school friend's family.

Her friend's parents had thought nothing of the children

spending all day in their swimming togs, playing on the shore, scrambling over rocks, tumbling down dunes and getting covered in gritty sand that had to be shaken out of all her clothes and shoes when she got home. Her mother had despaired at the effect of sun and sand and salt water on her fine, flyaway hair, and had been dismayed at the spattering of freckles that despite sunscreen had speckled her nose.

But that holiday had been one of the happiest times of her life. She hadn't thought about it in years, and now the memory brought an odd mixture of remembered happiness and a poignant sense of something lost. Childhood, she supposed.

A breaker thudded against the rock, and tiny salt droplets flung into the air spattered wide and far and dusted her cheeks. She wiped them with a hand and said, "Shouldn't we get back?"

"Are you in a hurry?" Jase asked.

"You said the tide's coming in."

"It won't be cutting us off yet, but if you're nervous…" He shrugged and began walking back across the rock, turning his head to check on her as she followed.

Reaching the edge where he'd helped her to climb up, she saw it was too far down to jump, and searched for an easier way. Jase went first, then looked up at her as she peered at the rock face for places to put her feet.

She made her decision and turned, feeling with her foot for a depression not far from the top. Then another. On the third one she slipped, lost her handhold and almost fell, then felt Jase's strong arms about her waist.

For an instant her back was pressed against his warm, hard chest, his lower body cradling hers, before her feet touched the sand and he loosened his hold. "Okay?"

"Yes. Thanks." She moved away quickly, and bent to

remove her shoes again. For a moment she had wanted to stay in the circle of his arms, lean back against him and…wait for whatever might come next.

She hadn't been held close by a man for a very long time. Maybe it was a primordial reaction, female hormones responding to a male embrace, even an accidental one that had no sexual intention.

Straightening, she sneaked a look at Jase. He was staring at the sea, thumbs thrust into the waistband of his jeans. His gaze swivelled to her and his eyes met hers with a dark, implicit question in them. Shaken, she realised she hadn't been the only one affected. Donning a carefully blank expression, she turned away from him and began to walk back the way they'd come.

Blind, instinctive attraction was no basis for an intimate relationship. The primitive sexual undertow below the surface was something neither of them really wanted. It was the unacknowledged source of the edginess that marked their every interaction, even when they stuck strictly to business. But whatever capricious mating instinct was produced between two people and their individual hormones, on every other level the unpredictable, abrasive, discomforting Jase Moore was simply not her type. Nor she his.

She veered close to an incoming wave, letting it gush over her feet as she pulled up the legs of her jeans to wade in the cold, shallow water. Jase picked up another piece of driftwood and hurled it over the crest of the next wave, then sent a small piece of rock after it.

The rock sank instantly, but the driftwood floated seaward until it was swallowed in a breaker, only to reappear farther out.

The rock would remain hidden under the sea, eventually

buried in sand, while the deceptively insubstantial driftwood might journey on the waves for years before reaching a foreign shore. Samantha was absently watching where it had disappeared when a rogue wave rushed across the receding ripples and caught her, soaking her jeans almost to her knees as, too late, she tried to escape, emitting a half-laughing squeal.

Jase was laughing too and she ruefully hurried away from the waterline, tossed her shoes aside and began trying to wring out the sodden denim.

He said, still smiling, "How about we find somewhere we can get a good meal?"

Samantha gave up on getting rid of the water, and cast him a disgusted look. "I'm not going anywhere looking like this!" She picked up her shoes and tried to maintain her dignity while struggling across the sand.

Her hair was tangled, her feet crusted with sand, and the legs of her jeans were rapidly acquiring more. Above the high tide mark she sank to the ankles on the dry, warm hillocks. The salty wind and spray had probably ruined her makeup too. She gave him a withering stare, and he laughed again. She wished he wouldn't—it made her want to forget all the reasons she hadn't given in to that silent invitation in his eyes at the rocks, hadn't stepped back into his arms and let natural instinct fly free of its cage.

When they reached his vehicle, Jase rummaged in the back for a towel. Samantha didn't ask its provenance, but although ragged at the edges and so faded its original colours were indecipherable, it looked reasonably clean. She rubbed sand from her feet as best she could, and brushed rather futilely at her jeans. Then she combed her hair and turned her back to do a rapid, inadequate repair job on her makeup.

When she settled herself into the passenger seat again he gave her a critical all-over glance and said, with a glimmer of laughter still in his eyes, "Feel better?"

"A bit. Considering I still must look like something the tide washed in."

Startling her, he put a hand under her chin and turned her face to his. The laughter faded. Almost roughly, he said, "You looked real—and alive—back there. Nothing wrong with that."

Before she could move, he lowered his head and kissed her, his lips firm, lingering only briefly on hers, slightly parted, subtly increasing the pressure on her mouth as if testing for her reaction.

She lifted her hand and pushed his light hold away, what he'd said still in her mind. As though he had the right to judge her, decide she was somehow less than fully human.

The seeming experimental nature of the kiss, and the way his too-penetrating gaze was obviously gauging her response now, added to her chagrin.

Did she normally look *un*real?

Sometimes she felt that way, as though she was playing a part, that the real Samantha Magnussen was hidden away from the world. Like the crabs in the rock pool, she had borrowed a hard shell that wasn't really hers so she could protect herself. Underneath was a soft, vulnerable being, hiding from attack, from exposure, pretending to be something it was not. If anyone penetrated her disguise she would die inside.

"I'm a woman," she said defensively, "in a man's world. It's all very well for you to go round looking like…the way you do."

"The way I do?"

"Um…casual."

"You mean scruffy." He didn't seem offended.

"I didn't say that." It was what she'd once thought, but the unruly hair and the chin-halo of his beard actually made him appear disturbingly male and sexy. "I just mean that I need to look professional if I want to be taken seriously."

He seemed to consider that. "It's still like that for women?"

"Some men think that because I'm female I'm not capable of running a company like Magnussen's. If I'd had a brother—"

She stopped abruptly and Jase said, "You're an only child, aren't you?"

"Yes. My father would have preferred a son, but he had to make do with me." Why had she blurted that out now? She'd never put it into words before.

Jase's gaze sharpened. "Did he say that?"

"He didn't need to." It was just something she'd known ever since she was barely school age, a conviction that became stronger as she grew older. No matter how much she tried to be what her father wanted she couldn't change her sex. She was never able to take the place of the son Fate had denied him.

She stirred, her eyes going to the low dunes with their sparse covering of tough, pale grasses and creeping plants. "Can we go now? I don't want to be too late getting home."

"Someone waiting for you?"

The question sounded idle, but she felt the razor-sharpness of his gaze.

"I have things to do," she said. "And my car's still parked at the office."

He nodded and started the engine.

They didn't speak much on the way back to the city. Samantha was preoccupied, thinking she should be careful what she said around this man. He had a knack of picking up on unguarded remarks, reading into them more than she'd expected or intended. And even the briefest of kisses set her pulse thundering and her body melting like chocolate in the sun.

She could still feel the warm pressure of his mouth on hers, and didn't dare wipe away the lingering, too-pleasant taste of it while he sat beside her.

It meant nothing, she told herself. A casual, spur-of-the-moment kiss that he might have given to any woman he'd spent a pleasant, leisurely hour or two with. He'd probably forgotten it already. Certainly he'd shown no sign of being upset by her rejection. And *that* was no reason for a niggling irritation on her part.

When he drew up outside the Magnussen Building she said, putting a hand on the door latch, "Thank you for the beach, it was a nice ending to the day."

"I'll see you to your car," Jase said. And insisted, despite her protest that she would be quite safe. When she'd unlocked the car he leaned forward to open the driver's door, touched her cheek and said, "Take care."

The banal words somehow warmed her, the warmth lasting all the way home—until she entered the apartment and found it almost chilly. The sparse furniture in leather and metal that she'd chosen with care for its elegant design, durability and ease of cleaning now somehow appeared uninviting.

She showered off the sand and put on a short silk nightgown, and an embroidered kimono she'd bought on a business trip to Japan, then microwaved a piece of chicken and made a small salad to go with it.

She felt alive and alert and after her shower rather mellow. A feeling of wellbeing she hadn't experienced for a long time.

That it was due to Jase Moore was peculiar, considering what he'd thought of her—possibly still did. He'd never retracted his initial assumptions and he'd been openly sceptical of her denials.

The nature of the kiss still bothered her—what had he been trying to find out exactly?

Not that his opinion of her mattered, of course. So long as he did his job and fulfilled his contract with Magnussen's that was all she needed from him.

It wasn't the thought that now they'd finalised his proposal they'd be working less closely that caused a sudden dip in her mood. Of course not.

Driving to his country home after dropping her off, Jase reminded himself that, spurred by the shock of learning she'd made Bryn a member of her board, he'd taken on the Magnussen's project because it would help him keep an eye on Samantha.

Working with her, he'd briefly, rarely, seen glimpses of a softer, warmer and much more vulnerable being than the one she presented to the world.

And today she'd been…different again. Enjoying the simple pleasure of sea and sand and rock pools filled with secret life; unselfconsciously paddling in the waves, and laughing at her own discomfort when the cross-current caught her unawares. She didn't lack a sense of humour.

Kissing her had seemed not only natural but necessary. He'd taken a calculated risk, that it might make her let down her guard so he could find out what she was hiding underneath it, what made her tick. The more he saw of Samantha Magnussen, the more he'd had a driving need to melt the ice and find the real woman beneath.

But she'd rejected his kiss and retreated physically and emotionally, shutting him out again.

Her privilege, and anger wasn't an appropriate response, he told himself.

By the time he'd returned her to her car, her customary unbendable composure was back in place, exasperating him further.

What would he have to do to get to the real, living, breathing, passionate creature he sensed behind the impenetrable surface gloss? Somewhere inside there was a heart, he knew. A woman's heart that could be broken just like anyone else's. And perhaps had been.

After the first upheaval and major changes, and a couple of short-lived hitches, Jase's new systems proved to work as smoothly as he'd promised.

Samantha was able to home in from the computer on her desk to any of the company's building sites, and confer with the site manager on a large wall screen while zooming in on the particular area under discussion.

Jase himself supervised the installation in her office, although when it came time to load new programmes she vacated her chair and watched him install them.

She said, standing at his shoulder, "Still, there's nothing like actually being there. When are you geniuses going to add smell to this great technology? That's what I miss. The smell of turned earth and timber."

He laughed. "We're working on it. You can still go out on site and get mud on your shoes if you want to."

"That part I don't miss too much," she admitted. Although like everyone else she wore boots once actually on site.

"I could install voice commands for you now if you like," he said. "You'd never even have to touch the computer."

"I can't see myself sitting alone in my office and talking to a machine." She'd learned standard keyboard skills while taking her double degree in architecture and business studies, and practised until she could type as fast as she could think.

Jase said, "You don't need to use it if you don't want to."

"There's nothing wrong with my hands. Or my eyes."

"Nothing at all," he said. Half turning, he took her left hand and ran his thumb over the back of the smooth, pale skin, and as her startled eyes met his gaze she felt a sudden fierce tug of desire, saw the same in his. "Topaz," he murmured.

"What?"

"I saw a ring with a stone that colour, once. Blue topaz. Clear as glass and very beautiful."

A taut silence sizzled between them, filled with unspoken questions. His black brows lifted slightly.

No! She dragged her gaze from his knowing stare, pulled away her hand. It wouldn't do.

And immediately following that thought came another. *Why not?*

Because…because he wasn't her type. And he was Bryn's brother-in-law.

So? Temptation jeered, as Jase, his mouth firming, shrugged and turned back to the keyboard. Bryn was married, and she'd dealt with that. There was only the occasional twinge of envy of his wife, a tiny remnant of regret that the man who'd seemed perfect for her hadn't been interested. She wasn't spending her life mourning lost chances.

So why pass up this one?

A chance…of what? A red-hot affair with Jase Moore?

It was something she'd never had. She had been late venturing into sex, as a teenager made wary by her girlfriends' roller-coaster plummets from starry-eyed infatuation to heart-broken despair. She had worked too hard at being in command of her feelings to let some hormone-driven adolescent whim—or simple curiosity—endanger that control.

When later she decided the time had come she chose her first lover with care. While she found the experience pleasant, sex had never been something she couldn't resist. Eventually they parted without rancour. Of the few men allowed into her bed since, none had made it to a long-term relationship.

One she'd thought might do so had told her she was married to her business. Although he had a business of his own, one of many things they had in common, he resented sharing her time, and eventually found another lover who was willing to accept the role of mistress, at his beck and call. It strengthened Samantha's determination to make her career the centre of her life. That was something solid that would always be there so long as she kept it in good heart, something she could control.

No man had impinged on her self-image as a person in charge of her own life, her own business, her own emotions.

Until Jase. Standing beside him now, not even looking at him, her eyes firmly fixed on the big screen that showed a series of commands and options, she was achingly aware of his every small movement, even his breathing. Every nerve ending knew exactly how close he was—tantalisingly close yet not touching. But wanting to.

She kept watching the screen until her eyes watered.

When he'd finished and stood up, so close that she instinctively moved back two steps, fighting a desire to touch him, tempt him, give in to desire, she blurted out the only thing that came to mind. "You don't really still work from your parents' garage?"

His business card gave an e-mail address, an 0800 number, a Hamilton box number and an Auckland "Sales and Showroom" address. She knew he employed at least a couple of dozen people. It wasn't a small operation.

He gave her his pirate's grin, that lethal combination of macho magnetism and underlying ruthless purpose. "I'll take you to see it if you like," he offered, apparently casual, one thumb tucked into the waistband of the jeans he wore. "We could drive down to the Waikato at the weekend, have lunch with my parents and spend the day. You might even enjoy yourself."

The last was delivered so ironically she was immediately on the defensive. "I'm sure I would." And sure he hadn't meant it, looking forward to watching him try to wriggle out of his own trap now she'd called his bluff.

Instead he said promptly, "How about this coming weekend."

"I'm going to a christening party on Sunday."

The glint lighting the depths of Jase's eyes held hidden laughter. "Saturday then," he said decisively.

Surely the suggestion had been an impulse he must have instantly regretted. Only he wouldn't back down once he'd made it.

Or maybe—just maybe, it was an olive branch, a sign he'd finally decided that she wasn't, after all, the unscrupulous Jezebel he'd imagined.

Unless…unless he wanted to explore the unasked-for spark that hovered in the air between them. If that was in his mind, it would change everything.

The thought made her heart flip, and warmth uncurl in her midriff.

No, she reminded herself yet again. Instinct told her that Jase Moore was the one man who could wreck her carefully organised life, tear her heart apart, expose the quivering nerves of past hurts to renewed pain. Who would willingly invite all that?

He was too…too much. Too smart, too perceptive, too blunt. And too damned sexy.

Too dangerous.

CHAPTER SIX

THEY drove south on Saturday. Samantha had thought of cancelling the arrangement, but he'd see through her excuse and she wouldn't allow him to use any chink in her armour.

After one comprehensive perusal of the light-blue cotton shirt and the jeans that snugged her hips, Jase led her to a white car with the name of his company on the side, not the 4WD he used for site visits.

If underlying his casual, relaxed manner she sensed a hidden tension in the set of his mouth and the line between his brows as he concentrated on his driving, perhaps it was due to her own pent-up feelings.

She was acutely aware that entering into his world might be a rash step too far. And she was still unsure why he'd suggested it. If he'd hoped to explore their tenuous relationship— the thought made her heart skip a beat, and she tried to put it out of her mind. *Don't cross that bridge until you come to it.* Or more wisely, refuse to cross it.

They left the city and traversed the Bombay hills to descend to the green landscape of the Waikato. Samantha found the browsing dairy cows in their paddocks, the white sheep dotting distant hills and the wide, shading trees about the farmhouses rather restful. It was a change to have someone else drive so she could enjoy it.

When they reached the Maori King's hometown of Ngaruawahia where the Waikato River ran deep, dark and slow alongside the road, she let out a sigh as the last tension seemed to leave her body.

Jase shot her a look as he slowed for a troop of teenagers sauntering across the road. "What's that about?"

"Nothing," she said, and settled further into her seat. "I haven't been down this way for a while. I'm enjoying the countryside."

Stepping up speed as the sleepy little town began to recede behind them, he said, "I like it."

"That's why you still work from your parents' farm?"

"Just a country boy at heart," he said. "And from there to my Auckland office is not much over an hour's commute. The best of both worlds. The advantage of the computer age is being able to work anywhere you want."

But Samantha saw his slight frown deepen as he returned his attention to the road. "What's wrong?" she queried, wondering if he was regretting his impulse to invite her.

The frown disappeared. "Nothing." He echoed her earlier answer. "It's a nice day for a drive with a pretty girl by my side. What could be wrong?"

"I'm not a girl."

He took his eyes from the road again for a second. "A beautiful woman, then."

"Flattery?" She cast him a dry glance. "That's a change, from you."

"Not flattery. It's the truth."

From him, she almost believed he meant it. He'd certainly

never gone out of his way to pay her fulsome compliments. She looked at him, stupidly pleased that he thought her beautiful.

He was looking straight ahead through the windscreen as in front of them a large truck barrelled along at 20ks below the speed limit.

Jase accelerated and the speedometer needle crept up as they passed the truck before he pulled into line behind a row of cars.

Lapsing into silence, Jase tried to concentrate on his driving. He'd told himself to tread carefully today.

The invitation had been impulsive, but the more he saw of her, the more he wanted to really know her in every way—not just physically, although that thought stirred his body and sent the blood racing in his veins, but what she thought, what she felt, why she was so determined to lock her innermost self away from him and, he suspected, everyone else. Except maybe Bryn. How much had she been prepared to reveal to him?

Jase knew damn well that far from cutting Bryn from her life, she seemed to go out of her way to keep him close. Meeting him at the seminar might have been chance, but inviting him onto her board of directors was a deliberately provocative move.

It was after she'd let that bit of information slip that Jase asked his brother-in-law the question he'd been debating within himself for far too long, reluctant to challenge Bryn and possibly have Rachel find out. Samantha's name had come up in the conversation and he took his opportunity. "Do you two have a history?" he demanded. He'd been invited to dinner at Rivermeadows, and they were enjoying a beer on the terrace while Rachel helped Pearl prepare the meal.

Bryn frowned, apparently at a loss. "I've known Samantha for a long time, but not really well until after her father died and we became good friends."

"How good?"

Bryn looked surprised, then angry, and finally said crisply, "If you're getting at what I think you are, Jase, I resent the question. One, it's none of your damn business. Two, even if you were right, whatever happened before I married Rachel isn't anyone's business. And three, I would never cheat on your sister. I have the greatest respect and liking for Samantha Magnussen, and that's all I have to say about her."

Bryn had been born to money and prestige, and this was one of the few occasions Jase had seen him mount his high horse, telling the peasants where they stood. Maybe he should have tugged his forelock and apologised for his temerity.

Instead, seeing from Bryn's formidably closed mouth that there was nothing to be gained from persisting, he'd just grunted and let it slide.

Perhaps Samantha had accepted that his marriage put Bryn beyond her reach.

And perhaps, a cynical whisper suggested, he was trying to fool himself into believing that because of an increasingly powerful urge he had to take her to bed, to make love to her until she was stripped of all pretence, naked and defenceless in his arms.

Quite possibly his unruly libido was scrambling his brain.

Huntly blurred by—rows of small neat houses built for the coalminers who were part of the town's history—then they were in the countryside again until, not long before the highway reached the provincial city of Hamilton, Jase turned the car onto a side road that wound into low hills. Within ten minutes they were arriving at a post-and-rail fence with a wide gateway. The car rattled over a steel-pipe cattle stop and along a tree-lined driveway, coming to a stop outside a long, low brick house, double doors at one side indicating an internal garage.

As Samantha stepped out of the car she could see on a nearby ridge a classic, white painted weatherboard house, a wide veranda hung with wisteria spanning the front. The window frames, front door and corrugated-iron roof were marigold-yellow. It must be the original homestead.

Beside and slightly behind it stood a large outbuilding, also white and yellow, the triangle under its pitched roof filled with glass that glinted in the sun, part of a satellite dish peeking above the roof towards the back.

The door of the newer house in front of her opened and a tall, heavily built man with greying dark hair came out to greet them.

Mr Moore shrewdly assessed her with eyes very like his sons', took her proffered hand in a powerful, calloused grip and ushered her inside to meet his wife, who had short-cropped greying black hair, smooth light tan skin and Rachel's brown eyes. She smiled warmly at Samantha, saying, "I remember seeing you at Rachel's wedding." She kissed Jase and, refusing help in the kitchen, sent them off to the big, comfortable sitting room to have a drink before lunch.

Minutes after they had settled in the spacious, comfortable front room there was a bang on the outer door, and moments later Ben and his wife entered. "Gidday!" He beamed at Samantha, and his wife, now pregnant and glowing with it, greeted her with a soft smile.

The energy in the room seemed to increase with their advent. Ben joshed his brother, and Jase returned the teasing. Their mother, who had joined them, sighed and shook her head, but with a smile on her lips. She was obviously fond of April too, the quiet young Filipina who carried her first grandchild.

They accepted Samantha into their midst, including her in the conversation, showing genuine interest in her answers to their questions about her job, her family, and expressing shock and sorrow that she had no one left.

"That must be hard for you," Mrs Moore said. "All alone with so much responsibility." Turning to Jase, she said, "You'd better take good care of this girl, Joseph."

Joseph? Samantha almost choked on the remains of her wine. She'd assumed Jase was short for Jason.

"I don't need taking care of," she said, not looking at him. "And we're just business…associates. Jase brought me down here to see his office, that's all. It's kind of you to give me lunch."

Everyone else in the room looked at Jase. Samantha could feel his eyes on her but kept her own gaze on the glass in her hand.

Mrs Moore broke the silence. "It's a pleasure," she said, getting up from her chair. "And lunch is ready."

After a meal of hearty quiche accompanied by a salad made with vegetables fresh from the garden outside, and followed by still-warm scones and home-made jam, no one seemed in a hurry to leave the large pinewood table.

Second cups of coffee were poured, and drunk over chat and laughter, until Ben said he had work to do, and reluctantly pushed back his chair. Everyone helped to put away food and take the dishes to the dishwasher, then Ben and April left to walk up the rise to the old homestead, where they lived.

Jase thanked his mother, gave her a kiss and said, "I'm taking Samantha to see my office."

They left by the back door and as they followed the dirt

and shingle driveway to the barnlike building Samantha had noted earlier, she said, "How does Joseph become Jase?"

"I never liked Joseph much, or Joe."

No, she couldn't see him as Joe.

"When I was about twelve," he said, "I decided using my initials was cool, and it sort of morphed from that."

They arrived at the big building and he placed his thumb on a tiny square beside the yellow doors, which silently swung open.

Jase ushered her in ahead of him, and she stepped into what she supposed was a high-tech heaven, and within seconds the doors had just as silently closed behind them.

"This is it," he said. "Where my development team works."

High strip windows lit a large space filled with electronic paraphernalia and computer screens of all sizes. Cables snaked along the walls, above wide benches on which sat an array of keyboards and computer mice and personal printers. A couple of free-standing desks also held computers and various folders, there was a huge printer and copier in one corner, and drafting tables occupied most of the remaining space, leaving a broad passageway down the middle of the carpeted floor.

At the other end of the big room Jase opened a door into a passageway leading to toilet facilities and a kitchen, staff-room and a meeting room with big windows showing a paved area outside shaded by trees. Several outdoor tables and chairs occupied the courtyard.

As they turned back to the main space Samantha said acer-bically, "Your parents' garage?"

"I had it converted, extended and built a second floor. But it's where I started, and the rent helped my mother get the house of her dreams. Farmers tend to plough their profits back into the land, and my father kept putting off building the new home he'd promised her when they bought this place. Now he's semi-retired, Ben and April are share-milking and eventually they'll take over the farm."

"You're a very close-knit family." She'd felt cocooned in their collective warmth ever since stepping into his parents' home.

"We get on," he said. "We all have our own lives, but even when Rachel was away overseas, she phoned home every week and sent e-mails to keep in touch."

He indicated a stairwell between the staff quarters and a wall. "And this is where I live. I have a place in Auckland too but here is what I think of as home."

Upstairs, after opening another door with his thumbprint on the little electronic pad, he showed her a kitchen, practical with stainless steel and hardwearing surfaces, a small table and two chairs tucked into a window corner.

An alcove in a short, wide passageway held a digital washing machine and dryer with a stainless steel washtub. A large tiled bathroom was dominated by a huge tub and a separate shower that boasted plenty of elbow room—enough for two, Samantha privately surmised, or even more. For a second she wondered if he ever used it with company—female company. What would it be like to stand under a shower like that with Jase?

Quickly she buried the wayward thought and instead studied the long marble counter and wide inbuilt washbasin.

Everything was unfussy, but obviously the best materials and craftsmanship had contributed to the deceptively simple luxury. She could have costed it to within a few hundred dollars. This radical makeover of an old though solid building hadn't come cheap. Jase knew where to spend his money wisely, on people who knew their job and took pride in their work.

"I'm impressed," she said. "Who was the architect?"

He laughed. "Part of what I do for other people is draw up floor plans. This one's pretty basic. I did some of the carpentry too."

The room next door seemed dim and shadowy until Jase pressed a button by the door and a blind attached to the ceiling opened, revealing a large skylight that flooded the space with sunshine.

A Pacific Island cotton print covered a king-size bed, swirling black patterns over a red-brown background. A luxurious black-leather sofa occupied a corner, and solid wood panels, one with a full-length mirror inset, hid what she presumed was a built-in wardrobe. A long counter with drawers underneath served as a dressing table, with a mirrored wall behind it, but at the other end of the counter near a window sat a computer, a typing chair pushed into a knee space below. Even in his bedroom, apparently, Jase had to have a computer handy.

As if he read the thought, he said, "Sometimes an idea or a solution to a problem comes to me in the middle of the night."

She noticed the jade abacus she remembered him buying had also found a place near the computer.

Despite being spacious, there was an air of intimacy in the room. She could imagine Jase relaxing here, sprawled on the expansive bed with a book—or a lover.

That didn't bear thinking of. She stepped over to the abacus and touched one of the carved beads with a finger, willing her mind away from carnal speculations as Jase walked to the bed and touched a button on a pad over the plain wooden headboard.

With a faint whirr the skylight opened, sending fresh, warm air into the room. "I like to lie here looking at the sky on a starry night," he said. "You don't see that in the city. Sometimes I leave it open when I go to sleep."

Samantha pushed aside the picture of Jase lying on the bed, maybe naked or nearly so. "And if it rains?"

He laughed. "The first sign of moisture, it closes automatically."

There were lights of course, and music that wafted from some unseen source. He touched another control and the blind overhead began to unroll before he stopped it again. Another, and the head of the bed gently rose. "For reading. Or watching TV."

A square of wall opposite the bed lifted out of the way to display a TV screen set into the cavity. "A Japanese guy has developed a wallpaper that doubles as a screen," Jase said. "Not in time for me to use it here, and anyway mostly I have better things to do in bed than watch TV."

Samantha's eyes flickered away from the gleam in his, and he laughed softly. "Sleeping," he said. "Reading, using my laptop. Not what you're thinking, Samantha."

"I wasn't thinking anything," she informed him, looking him in the eye, daring him to contradict her.

"Of course not," he said, so soothingly she wanted to shake him. The gleam in his eyes intensified, and her body tautened as he approached her, but with his hand at her waist he walked her out of the bedroom and along the passageway towards the front of the building.

As if by some unseen hand, double doors ahead of them whispered open. Even as she passed through she had an impression of light and space, of entering into a non-earthly dimension.

A vista of green and blue, earth and sky drew her forward across a thick moss-coloured carpet to the huge triangle wall of glass that reached to the floor.

The road was hidden behind a screen of trees, and the countryside stretched for miles. Lush grass and dark, thick native trees were interspersed with splashes of colour in a few farm gardens—pink and purple, gold and red—all under the wide canopy of almost cloudless blue sky.

She caught a glimpse of water glittering in sunlight not too far away, and followed a line of trees that opened here and there to allow more tantalising peeks at a lazy, winding stream.

"Like it?" Jase asked at her side.

"How could your parents bear to leave it?"

"Gets windy up here," he said. "And they didn't want a two-storey house for their retirement years. It's only up this high that the view is worth it." He looked up, surveying the few ragged clouds scudding upward from the horizon. "If you stay until sunset, it could be a good one. Sometimes they're pretty spectacular."

"Sunset's a long way off." She looked at her watch, finding it already later than she'd thought. "What would we do in the meantime?"

Jase said, "I could think of a couple of things I'd like to do with you."

Her eyes flew to his face. Despite the lightness in his voice he wasn't smiling. And at the heat in his eyes her heart stuttered and her breath paused.

Involuntarily she took a step back—while she still could. Because every nerve she possessed was screaming at her to go forward into his arms, and fear of losing herself there kept her sane and cautious.

The air seemed full of electricity, crackling with it. She was conscious of the sunlight warming her face through the shimmering glass of the windows, the blinding blue of the sky outside, the softness of the carpet under her feet. In her mind, as if she were an onlooker, she could see herself and Jase facing each other, an arm's length apart, see the rise and fall of his chest under his shirt, hear the sound of his breathing.

She could have reached out and touched him. Wanted to.

Instead she turned to examine the room, taking in details she had only peripherally noticed.

Large and squishy navy-leather sofas formed a U-shape before that expansive view, bookshelves lined one wall, and on another was a long Maori taiaha—sharply pointed at one end, tasselled at the other, intricately carved along the shaft. Below it hung a large framed map, obviously old—or pretending to be. She moved closer, away from Jase and temptation, and saw the map represented an island, with curlicued legends all around and sailing ships anchored in the harbours.

"New Providence," Jase said. When she looked around he was standing where she'd left him, hands jammed in his pockets, his expression stone-carved but his eyes watchful. "The island was a hangout for pirates in the seventeenth century. Part of my first commercially successfully game is based on the place."

"It's genuine?" She peered at the date on one corner. "Sixteen ninety-nine?"

"According to the expert I got to check it. Might even have come off a real pirate ship."

"Why did you choose to write pirate games?" she asked, turning back to him.

"Robert Louis Stevenson," he answered. "*Treasure Island.* After we read the book Ben and Rachel and I played pirate games around the farm—not this one...my father was managing the Donovans' estate farm then—and in the Donovans' garden. It was a great place for kids."

"Rachel? Playing pirates?"

"The most bloodthirsty of the lot." His stance became a little less rigid, a faint smile playing around his mouth. "And adventurous—the kid didn't know the meaning of fear. Anything Ben and I did, she wanted to do too. We had to watch out for her all the time, and she still collected a fair number of cuts and scrapes and bruises."

"Really?" Rachel as a tomboy?

"Scared the wits out of us a couple of times." Jase's smile turned ruefully reminiscent. "There are things our parents to this day don't know. Apart from the fact we were actually quite fond of the little brat, Dad would have skinned us alive if we'd let anything serious happen to her."

Something twisted painfully inside her. Bizarrely, without right or reason, she was jealous of his *sister*. He'd obviously never grown out of the imperative to protect her. And "fond" was a deliberate understatement. He would willingly die for her if necessary. Without a doubt. She was family, and that was all Jase needed to give his unstinting loyalty and love.

He said, "It was Rachel who started getting library books about real pirates. That's what sparked her interest in history. And mine, although I didn't make a career of it."

"That's how you came to invent pirate games?" she said.

"What else was I going to do with all that information once I got hooked on computers? Interestingly, piracy in the so-called Golden Age was really all about economics and trade wars, supply and demand. You might appreciate that. I made the games as authentic as possible. Most of the characters and events in them are real."

"Educational games?"

"Primarily they're for fun." He shrugged. "If people learn from them, it's a side effect."

"I've never seen your games," she confessed. "I only use computers for work."

He shook his head as though she were some kind of freakish, previously unknown specimen. "Sit down over there."

He picked up what looked like a TV remote, and one of the sofas in the U swung aside and lined itself up against another, leaving a clear space between a solid, square coffee table and a large screen in the wall like the one in his bedroom. He used the same gadget to light up the screen.

For the next hour and a half she became a Spanish sea captain trying to get a cargo of gold and gems from the Atlantic coast of America to the mother country, while warding off a horde of swashbuckling, rip-roaring pirates.

At first Jase helped her, patiently explaining what to do. She found it easy enough to follow his instructions and soon got the idea. She knew he was holding off at first, letting her get the hang of the game, but once she managed to disable the pirate ship with a direct hit from her cannons, her competitive streak took over and she leaned forward in her seat, intent on using everything Jase had taught her in a determined effort to destroy the enemy.

Of course Jase won, but she had bloodied him and killed half his crew.

"Not bad for a beginner," he said as he leaned back after capturing the Spanish ship and surrounding her "avatar," alias the Spanish captain, with a bunch of fierce and victorious pirates. "I'm afraid your only choice now is surrender."

"Not on your life."

"It's *your* life that's at stake," he said.

"I won't give in. I'm sure the captain would accept death rather than give up his ship."

"He's already lost that," Jase pointed out.

"But not his self-respect. Go on. Do your worst."

Jase lounged in a corner of the sofa, his eyes alert and watchful beneath half-closed lids. He said softly, "I don't want to put a sword through your heart, Samantha."

CHAPTER SEVEN

HIS lopsided grin was teasing, but effortlessly sexy, and his tone had changed. Samantha met his eyes, saw unmistakable desire in them and her heart took a startled leap into her throat.

She swallowed, then said huskily, "Aren't you supposed to give me a chance? Set me adrift in a ship's boat or something?"

He laughed, a little ruefully, and the heat left his eyes. "Pirates were a pretty ruthless lot. Is a slow death by starvation and thirst better than a quick one by the sword?" He pressed a switch and the screen went blank. He said, "It's a nice day outside. We could take a walk across the farm. There's a bit of bush, with a waterfall and a deep pool. We could even swim if you like."

"I don't think so."

"It'd be quite safe, I promise."

Safe? Nothing about being with Jase Moore felt safe. "Thanks, but no thanks."

"Afraid of getting out of your depth?" His eyes challenged her.

"I didn't think you were serious—about swimming."

He laughed again at her evasion. "A walk then," he said. "Are you up for that?"

She should say no, tell him she wanted to go home. Back

to the city and her apartment where she could close herself off in her own small world. Where no one dared her to step outside her comfort zone and into new experiences, or delved behind the surface of her carefully cultivated social face to stir up the emotions beneath.

Yet something held her, a feeling that maybe she'd regret taking the coward's way out.

Perhaps sensing her ambivalence, Jase said, "It'll be good for you. Country air."

Jase took her hand to help her over a stile that spanned an electrified fence. He kept his fingers wrapped around hers as they skirted cowpats and tiny blue and salmon-pink wild-flowers peeking through the grass. She didn't object. The ground was uneven and she didn't want to trip and make a fool of herself. And, honesty whispered, she liked the feel of his strong hand holding hers.

He paused to attack a thistle with the heel of his boot, cutting it off ruthlessly at the root. He'd been brought up on farms and she supposed such things were second nature to him. A wind had sprung up, lifting Samantha's hair from the back of her neck, and blowing it round her face. She put a hand up to clear her eyes.

A grazing herd of white-faced black cattle stopped to stare in a solid phalanx at the intruders walking past. They looked so comical that Samantha laughed, still trying to deal with her hair. Jase smiled down at her and his hand tightened slightly on hers.

Eventually they entered a gully fenced off from the pasture land, their footfalls silent on moss and fallen leaves under trees growing thick and dark green beside a narrow path, cutting the wind. The sound of rushing water grew louder until they reached a shallow stream strewn with big, smooth stones, the water leaping and foaming around them and then abruptly sliding over a rocky ledge.

Jase led her on a steep downhill path to the pool below the falls, and they stood so close to the plunging water that fine droplets of spray cooled Samantha's face.

Something long and black and sinuous stirred in the water at their feet and she backed up instinctively, but Jase had her hand firmly in his. "Just an eel," he said.

Samantha suppressed a shudder. "And you suggested swimming?"

"Nothing's going to hurt you here," he said. "I promise." Abruptly he took a couple of steps away from her, dropping to the coarse grass at the water's edge and sitting with one leg straight out in front of him as he rested a forearm on the other knee. "Why don't you sit down?" he said, indicating the grass beside him.

Samantha hesitated, then sat down nearby but not too close, wrapping both arms about her raised knees.

A tui somewhere in the trees nearby sent a few rich, contralto notes into the air, followed by its distinctive throaty gurgle, as though mocking its own song. A couple of tiny fantails flirted nearby, swooping and darting. Something jumped from the water in a flash of silver and twisted back with a small splash.

"Was that a trout?" Samantha asked, startled.

"There're a few of them around." Jase shifted his position, leaning on one forearm as he turned to see her face. "Ever been fishing?"

"I like my fish cooked and on a plate, not wriggling on a hook. I suppose that means I'm a hypocrite, but some things I prefer not to think about."

"So don't."

"It isn't always that easy."

"Tell me about it!" he said under his breath. Then, "What are you thinking about now?"

She evaded his eyes, the lazy curiosity in them. "Nothing, except how peaceful it is here." She returned her gaze to the hypnotically rushing water endlessly hurling itself over the rock face. Jagged shards of sunlight danced through the trees onto the surface of the pool.

Jase watched her profile, the line of her nose, the long lashes that brushed her cheek when she blinked, the curve of her mouth, and the sun glinting on her hair, which had fallen back into its sleek style, to gently brush along her chin. He had a powerful urge to pull her down beside him and make love to her, bury his fingers in her sun-warmed hair, see those almost translucent blue eyes widen and darken, feel her skin heat beneath his hands, her firm but enticingly feminine mouth open for him.

It wouldn't happen. For one thing, she'd made it clear she wasn't interested. And for another...did she still carry a torch for Bryn?

The thought made him angry, and it was time to quit fooling himself that the anger, smouldering away like white-hot coals inside him for months, was all on his sister's behalf. The brutal truth was he wanted Samantha for himself. Sometimes he was sure she wasn't as indifferent as she pretended. Or—he considered the alternative—he was an arrogant fool, deceiving himself.

The thought of her opening her heart to the other man—any other man—made Jase's fists curl.

He said, just to capture her attention, try to gauge her mood, "Tell me when you've had enough."

For a moment she didn't respond, and when she looked at him briefly her eyes seemed dreamy, as if it wasn't him she saw but something inside herself. "Not yet. Unless you want to go," she said and, when he shook his head, she resumed staring at the water.

His fingers closed around a grass stalk, snapped it from its root. What he wanted to do right now was grab hold of Samantha and kiss her senseless. For a start. For a few moments he enjoyed the thought processes that followed that.

Watching the waterfall, she was apparently oblivious to everything else, including him.

Throwing down the piece of grass he'd mangled, Jase sat up. Samantha turned to him and blinked, as if just remembering his presence. Which didn't improve his mood. If he'd followed his primal instincts, she'd have damn well noticed him, had something to remember. Maybe he should do it. Find out once and for all if that sexual spark he suspected she was trying to snuff out could be fanned into a consuming flame. The very idea made his body react. He moved restlessly.

"Do you want to leave?" she asked.

"No." What he wanted wasn't an option. He'd promised she'd be safe. And whatever she was so afraid of, he knew it included any sexual advances from him. He stood up and strolled away from her, pretending to get a better view of the falls.

Finally Samantha sighed and stood up. The sun had lowered, and as they retraced their steps through the trees the light grew dimmer. They spoke little and Jase merely took her arm a few times when the going was rough.

Entering his apartment again, Samantha saw he'd been right about the sunset. The edges of the clouds were shining gold, and while she and Jase watched from the big window the sun sank lower, turning the clouds fiery red.

As the colours faded from the sky, Jase said, "Sit down and I'll get us something to eat."

"You didn't invite me for dinner," she protested. "You don't have to feed me again."

"Aren't you hungry? I am. Unless you'd rather stop at a restaurant on the way…"

"No, we'll eat here if you don't want to wait. Can you cook?"

Jase laughed. "It might not be haute cuisine, but I can rustle up something."

"I'll help."

"Nope. Trust me. You like rice?"

"Yes."

"Prawns?"

"Yes."

"Good," he said. "I'll bring you a glass of wine to enjoy while I get dinner. White or red?"

She asked for white, and as he left the room he clicked his fingers and muted music—light classical—filtered into the room. It took her minutes to spot the discreet speakers inset into the ceiling. More of his computerised gadgetry.

He brought in a bottle and a glass, and after pouring for her left the bottle. Te Mata Elston Chardonnay, she noted. Not a cheap wine.

Presently, as the shadows drew in around the corners of the room, a lamp automatically came on beside the sofa where she'd been leafing through a copy of *Science* magazine, and when delicious aromas began coming from the kitchen she realised she *was* hungry.

Drawn by curiosity, she put the magazine aside, poured herself a second glass of Chardonnay, picked up the bottle and went to the kitchen door. Steam rose from a pan on the state-of-the-art cooker, and Jase was laying cutlery on a small table in the corner.

He looked up and said, "You don't mind eating here?"

Samantha shook her head. "No." It looked rather… intimate but she could hardly object on that ground. "Are you sure there's nothing I can do?"

He nodded to a tray on the counter holding salt, pepper and three sauces. "Put those on the table if you like."

She arranged the condiments on the table and Jase said, "Sit. It's ready."

He brought two plates and placed one in front of her. "The prawns were frozen," he said, "but fresh out of the sea when they went into the freezer."

Samantha tasted one from the top of the pile of rice and vegetables on her plate. "It's delicious," she told him. The rice was subtly spiced and equally good.

Jase picked up a bottle of Kaitaia Fire chilli sauce and poured it liberally over his rice.

"That'll burn the roof of your mouth off!" Samantha said, watching.

"I like it hot," Jase answered. "A bit of spice in your life won't do any harm."

"*My* life?"

He looked up, a pink prawn on the end of his fork. "Anyone's," he said. "Including yours."

Samantha looked down at her rice, stirring it. "You don't know anything about my life."

"Want to tell me?"

"No." She forked up a mouthful of rice, an excuse not to say more.

Jase shrugged, and turned his attention to his own food.

For a while they ate in silence, sipping at their wine, then he said, "Have you enjoyed yourself today?"

"Yes," she said, unable to keep surprise from her reply. "Very much."

He finished the last few grains on his plate and said, "Will cheese and fruit do instead of dessert?"

"That would be nice, thank you."

He watched her scoop up the rest of her rice and put her fork down. "You'd say that anyway," he said, "wouldn't you? You've been properly brought up."

"And you haven't?" she countered.

"My mother tried. It's not her fault it didn't take."

She said, "There's nothing wrong with your manners." He actually had a better grasp of the courtesies than many men. He opened doors for her, had made sure she didn't trip on the unfamiliar stairs, and when they walked over the farm had steered her around the cowpats and rough ground. "I'm sure your mother's proud of you."

"I hope so." He pushed back his chair and took her plate, to place it with his own in the dishwasher before opening the refrigerator.

He put three cheeses before her on a platter, and presented a bowl of apples, pears and grapes. "Sorry, I'm out of crackers."

"This is fine." She picked up the cheese knife and cut a sliver of Kapiti Kahurangi Blue. Rich and creamy, not too strong, it melted on her tongue. "Mmm," she said appreciatively, savouring the taste before picking up her wine, to find the glass already three-quarters empty.

When she put it down Jase refilled it, not for the first time, and she didn't protest. While he cut himself a generous wedge of blue, she kept sipping at the wine, nibbled a couple of grapes and chose a piece of marigold-coloured hard cheese. "What's this?" she asked.

"Aged Gouda from the Mahoe cheese factory up north."

She put it in her mouth and found it crunchy and utterly delicious. Momentarily she closed her eyes, the better to enjoy the flavour before swallowing. "It's *wonderful!*" she said reverently, reaching for another slice. "I haven't had this particular one before."

"You're a cheese buff?"

"I'm no expert, but I know a good cheese when I taste one."

"The other one's a vintage Cheddar," he said. "I buy most of my cheese from the Vintage Cheese Company at Mercer, on my way between here and Auckland. A pity it'll be too late when we head back up there. Unless you'd care to stay the night." His voice was casual.

She had picked up her wine again, but her hand stilled in midair. His eyes when she met them were dark and serious, his gaze steady.

Keeping her voice light, she asked, "Is that a proposition?"

"If you want it to be," he said. "Or you could have the bed and I'll take a sofa."

For a moment she had a vision of lying in that big bed, gazing up at the stars, with Jase at her side—after making love.

Carefully she put the almost empty glass back on the table. "I could get a taxi," she said, "if you don't want to drive back."

"It would cost a fortune. But you have one, don't you? What was it like, being a poor little rich girl?"

"I wasn't a poor little rich girl." Her voice was crisp. "And I'm not the only one worth a fortune. I hear you're close to joining the billionaires' club. And all your own work too," she added mockingly.

"A slight exaggeration. At least you know I'm not after your money."

"I didn't think you were after anything from me." Except a promise to keep away from his sister's husband. Or had they moved on from that? She wasn't sure.

He said, "Maybe you should think again."

Samantha blinked at the steady light in his eyes.

Jase got up, pushing back his chair, and she stiffened, all her nerves jumping to life. But he only turned away and opened a cupboard, taking down a jar to spoon coffee into a coffeemaker.

Unthinkingly Samantha grabbed at her glass and finished the wine in it. It should have made her feel better, but instead she realised she was a little giddy.

How many glasses had she had? Three in a little over an hour? Or had it been four?

She was usually more cautious. Hastily she ate another grape and reached for a chunk of cheddar.

"We'll have coffee in the other room," Jase said. "I'll join you there when I've made it, if you've had enough to eat."

Samantha stood up, glad he wasn't watching. She steadied herself on the back of her chair and then walked to the door. "I don't want to be too late getting home," she said as she paused. Just to make things clear. "I have a party to go to tomorrow."

"Okay, Cinderella," he said easily. "You'll be tucked up in your own bed before midnight."

If he had propositioned her, he was taking her refusal remarkably well, she thought with an irrational spurt of pique.

Jase watched her go, his hand tightening on the coffeepot as he placed it on the heating plate. He wanted to follow Samantha and like some caveman haul her by the hair—or any other part of her anatomy—into his bed.

When she'd disappeared from sight he put both hands on the counter in front of him and dropped his head, eyes closed.

She was the only woman who had ever awakened such primitive feelings. The only one he found so infuriatingly difficult to fathom.

He watched the drips falling into the glass jug and brooded. What was under all that glacial inaccessibility? She'd shown more emotion over a piece of *cheese* than she'd ever allowed him to dig out. When her mouth closed over it and her eyelids drifted down while her chin lifted at the taste, her expression had been the nearest thing to ecstasy. His imagination had instantly run riot with X-rated sexual fantasies.

His body had reacted predictably, and he'd had to turn his back and walk away to prevent himself from leaning across the table and grabbing her. This whole trip had been a test of his patience and self-control.

He'd hoped his boisterous, open family might break down some part of the icy shell.

If only he could get inside her head, her mind, her heart. If he could get her to trust him, tell him her real feelings.

The coffee machine seemed to be taking forever to percolate. Sugar. Samantha liked sugar in her coffee. He took a bowl of brown crystals from the cupboard, frowning at the centimetre or so of liquid left in the wine bottle, then lifted the coffee jug.

It was a long time since Samantha had seen so many stars. Here they weren't dimmed by city lights, although the distant glow near the horizon was presumably Hamilton. A few clouds were still around, and now and then one crossed the polished-copper full moon still low in the sky.

The music in the room had changed to a selection of easy-listening, once-popular hits from the previous century. Standing at the big window, unconsciously she began to sway in time to a dance tune her mother used to like. She remembered that once they'd danced to it together, holding hands, while her mother taught her the steps, pleased that Samantha easily picked them up.

A feeling for music and rhythm was one of the few things she'd inherited from her mother. Not Ginette's vividly sky-blue eyes, her pretty, heart-shaped face or her thick, lustrous strawberry-blonde hair, nor her natural charm and grace.

A gangly child with long limbs that seemed bony and out of proportion to her body, milk-skinned and naturally reserved, Samantha hadn't repaid her mother's efforts to dress her in frills and bows. Frills simply showed up her skinny legs and arms and featureless face with clear, almost transparent pale eyes, and ribbons slipped from her straight, colourless hair. Apart from dyeing it, a failed teenage experiment that for some reason had roused her father's ire, there was nothing she could do about her hair except ensure she had a very good hairdresser. A pity Ginette had never seen her late-blooming daughter grow into her awkward form, develop a decent figure and learn to make the most of her meagre assets.

But once, they had danced together and Samantha had earned her mother's praise.

The reflection behind her made Samantha realise Jase was back in the room, and she abruptly stopped moving.

As she turned, he straightened from putting a tray on the coffee table between the sofas.

He smiled at her and came over with his hand held out. "May I have this dance?" he said.

About to say she wasn't really dancing and only wanted coffee, Samantha was assailed by an uncharacteristic impatience with her own caution, a reckless what-the-hell feeling that was alien to her and almost frightening in its intensity.

She placed her hand in his and Jase put his arm about her and held her lightly, their bodies just touching, swaying to the music, moving in small steps.

He lifted his head to look at her, into her eyes. The circle of light around the sofa left the rest of the room only dimly lit, but his eyes held hers with a mysterious green glow, almost like a nocturnal big cat—a tiger, or a panther.

She stared back at him, mesmerised, thinking vaguely that she'd had too much wine too quickly—and this was dangerous, wasn't it? But that didn't abate the tingling throughout her body, the heat that flooded her veins, the dreamy, otherworldly mood that held her in thrall to the music, the night, and this unpredictable, abrasive, stunningly attractive man.

The music paused, and Jase stopped dancing but didn't release his hold on her. Samantha's heart momentarily stopped, too. Then a new track began, the strains of a lovesong filling the room, but instead of resuming the dance he just went on looking at her, unsmiling but with a question in his eyes. The same question she'd evaded earlier.

This time she didn't look away, and after a moment he lowered his head and nuzzled gently at her lips with his mouth.

Samantha stood perfectly still, as she would have on the brink of a cliff. Her eyes fluttered closed and she savoured the taste of his mouth, the feel of his arms tightening gradually around her, until he parted her lips with his and her head tipped back, her mouth opening further under his erotic persuasion.

Her hand on his shoulder moved to curve about his neck,

and she felt his hair, amazingly soft and silky, settle against her skin. Her other hand was held in his, over his heart, the beat of it sending pulsing thrills all the way to hers.

He explored her mouth, teasing, tantalising, tasting, until she kissed him back fiercely, pressing herself closer to him, feeling him react unmistakably to that, the kiss becoming even deeper-questing, demanding, until her body began to sing, taut as a stretched wire, silently screaming with tumultuous, raw need.

Finally he tore his mouth away from hers and said hoarsely, "Have you changed your mind about staying?"

For a moment she simply stared at him, not even comprehending the question.

Before she had a chance to answer, he shook his head as though trying to clear it, and loosened his hold on her. "Hang on," he said. "You taste of wine."

"That's a problem?" she asked dazedly.

"No…*yes*!" he said. "I think so. You drank most of the bottle."

"You drank—"

"One glass," he interrupted. "So I could drive you home. Which is what I'm going to do—" he drew in a harsh breath "—just as soon as you've had some coffee."

Then he let go of her, so suddenly that she swayed. Or the room did, before it righted itself.

"I'm not *drunk*!" she said.

"Just a bit tipsy," he agreed, his grin crooked. He took her arm in a firm grip and said, *"Coffee."*

CHAPTER EIGHT

THE journey back to Auckland in the dark seemed endless. Samantha stared through the windscreen, her back rigid. Jase drove with a ferocious concentration, a frown between his brows, occasionally allowing the speedometer to creep just beyond the speed limit, as if he couldn't wait to get rid of her.

Outside her apartment he flung wide the driver's door, going round the car and getting hers open before she had time to unclip the unfamiliar seatbelt and do it herself.

He walked her to the entrance of the building, watched her use her key and said, "You'll be all right now?"

"Of course." She tried to sound gracious. "Thank you for a nice day."

"Glad you enjoyed it." His voice was clipped. A short, awkward silence ensued; then he said in a muffled voice, "Good-night."

And was gone before she had closed the door behind her.

It wasn't fair to blame him, she knew, aware that he'd been chivalrous, unwilling to take advantage of a woman who'd had slightly too much to drink. That she found the fact humiliating wasn't his fault.

All the same, it was hard not to resent that Jase had been

the one to interrupt that kiss, just when for once she'd been on the brink of doing something hopelessly rash for a change, without weighing the consequences.

She would have pulled back, she assured herself. In another second or two. Perhaps three. Common sense would have prevailed. She ought to be grateful Jase hadn't followed through, considering she hadn't made the slightest effort to stop him. Hadn't wanted to.

It was only a kiss, after all.

And this tearing regret would surely be over by tomorrow, when she'd be stone-cold sober.

She wandered to her bedroom, suddenly very tired. Her movements slow, she stepped into the shower, the warm water cascading over her body reminding her of the shower in Jase's apartment and her earlier fantasy, shamefully erotic pictures dancing before her eyes. Abruptly she turned the shower to cold, gasping and shivering under the assault.

It didn't stop her dreaming about Jase after she climbed into her lonely bed. His body lightly touching hers while they danced, his eyes lit with desire, his mouth warm and persuasive against hers, his smile crooked and regretful when he pushed her away.

The dream left reality behind, and she felt his hands on her body, freed of clothing, saw herself running her fingers down his chest, stroking his hip, his thigh, kissing him in places she'd never kissed a man in reality.

Then he returned the compliment, touching, kissing everywhere, until he looked into her eyes again, lowered his body and…

Moaning with pleasure, she opened her eyes to darkness and emptiness.

She bit her lip, the aftermath of that phantom climax still

throbbing as it gradually faded, and she saw she had displaced the sheet, her short nightie rucked up, leaving her thighs exposed to the cooling night.

Damn Jase Moore. He'd awakened a craving that had never really bothered her before. And he was the wrong man to satisfy it. If she needed sex there were plenty of other men only too eager to offer it with no strings, no risk.

An affair with Jase would be fraught with complications. A relationship was probably the last thing he wanted. He might be attracted to her physically, but it had been far too easy for him to act the perfect gentleman. He was in no danger of losing his head over her.

After dropping off Samantha, Jase headed for his Auckland flat, calling himself all kinds of idiot. For not being able to keep his hands off her. For halting what might have been the perfect opportunity to breach her defences and get inside her—literally and figuratively, even the thought making him hot and hard. And for feeling that way about her in the first place.

All day he'd been trying to maintain some objectivity against the fantasies that kept entering his mind, trying to keep things light and not spook her into retreat. He'd told himself often enough that falling for Samantha Magnussen wasn't an option.

But when she looked at him that way, for once soft and vulnerable and accessible, he'd rationalised that one kiss wouldn't do any harm. He'd half expected her to push him away as she had the last time he'd kissed her.

Only she hadn't. Instead she'd melted into his arms and let him open her mouth to his, and...

And then for an instant, an aeon, he'd lost himself in the

feel of her body, so perfectly moulded to his, in the subtle perfume of her skin, her hair.

She'd tasted of wine, and that had finally penetrated the dim recesses of his brain, reminding him of the nearly empty bottle in the kitchen, of her un-Samantha-like mellow mood, of the way her eyes looked, gazing into his—sultry and slumbrous and inviting. Bedroom eyes.

Too-much-wine eyes.

She'd trusted him enough to drink more of his wine than was good for her, enough to make her drop some of her usual wary reserve. Enough to loosen her inhibitions. Maybe she'd even done it deliberately, knowing the effect it would have, waited for him to make a move.

And he had.

The perfect opportunity. And he'd blown it.

A red light brought him to a stop, drumming his fingers on the steering wheel, staring straight ahead at nothing while his brain went round and round on the same insistent, muddled track. He wasn't thinking straight, he knew. And it was due to the most maddening, intriguing, enigmatic woman he'd ever met.

A toot behind alerted him to the fact the light had turned green, and he moved the car forward, pressing the accelerator.

He should be feeling virtuous, having stuck to his principles; a decent man didn't take advantage of a drink-affected woman. Instead he felt frustrated and deep-down furious. Mostly with himself. Some part of him wanted to turn the car around and drive back to Samantha's apartment, kick down the door and carry on where they'd left off in his living room.

Maybe he wouldn't need to kick down the door. Maybe

she'd welcome him with open arms, drag him to her bedroom, take him to her bed. Where she probably was by now.

He slammed the door in his mind on a fantasy about what she'd be wearing in bed, how he'd remove it before…

A blinking orange light on the dashboard brought him back to reality. His petrol tank was showing low. He slowed and turned into the courtyard of a service station, glad of the distraction, although it didn't last long enough.

Despite a perfectly comfortable bed, he didn't sleep until the early hours of the morning. Once he'd showered and dressed he tried to phone Samantha with no reply, deciding not to leave a message on her answer machine. She must have already left for her Christening party.

Phoning wasn't a good idea anyway. He needed to see her face to face.

And say what? That he regretted he'd taken her home instead of to his bed? That he wanted to pick up where they'd left off? Either approach would send her scuttling back into her shell. It hadn't escaped him that she'd been chagrined when he'd broken off the kiss. She'd frozen him out from then on, no doubt feeling rejected.

Didn't she have any idea what acting like a gentleman had cost him? His mother would have been proud.

The trouble was, anything he said might make things worse. He'd never been famous for his tact. She might prefer not to discuss the incident at all.

Yes, that would be her style, he decided caustically. He should probably just leave her alone for a while until her embarrassment faded, let her get over it. Not the way he'd prefer—he'd been accused more than once of tackling personal problems like a bull at a gate—but he'd never met a woman quite like Samantha.

And while she was—hopefully—getting over it, maybe he'd come up with another plan of attack.

He spent all Monday at the Auckland office, itching to pick up the phone and telling himself to back off as he'd decided. After working until nine at night, he drove back towards Hamilton. On his arrival at the farm he was surprised to see Rachel's car outside his parents' new garage. He didn't think they'd been expecting her.

In the morning he decided to drop in for breakfast at the farmhouse and say hello to Rachel at the same time.

The minute he entered the kitchen at the back door he knew something was wrong. His mother looked upset as she stood at the toaster, and his father was scowling over his home-grown beef sausages and free-range eggs.

"What's happened?" he asked. "Rachel?"

His mother said, "In her room. She's staying for a few days." The toaster popped and she removed a couple of pieces. "Do you want breakfast?"

"Later," he said. "Is she all right?"

"She says she's left Bryn."

It felt like a punch in the gut. *"Why?"*

His father looked up. "She's not talking," he growled.

"I told her," his mother said, "all marriages hit rough patches, but…I don't know."

A feeling of foreboding had lodged in Jase's stomach. He touched his mother's arm, then left the kitchen to go down the hallway and knock on the door of the spare bedroom. "Rache?" Shortening her name as he had when they were kids. "You okay?"

"Go away, Jase," came the muffled reply. "I'm fine."

He snorted at that obvious untruth. "You'd better be decent because I'm coming in." He gave her a couple of seconds and then opened the door.

Rachel was sitting on the bed, wearing shorts and a baggy T-shirt. She tried to glare at him, but it didn't come off because her eyes were full of tears. She turned away to grab a handful of tissues from a box on the dressing table, and wiped her eyes and nose. "I said, go away!" she reiterated huskily.

"Hey," he said, "I just want to help. What the hell is going on? It's not like you to come running home to Mummy."

Her head rose defensively. "It's just until I find a place. Somewhere I won't bump into—" she swallowed a gulp "—into Bryn. But last night—this was the only place that felt safe."

"Safe?" Jase's hackles rose. "He didn't *hit* you? If he did I'll—"

"*No!* Bryn would *never* do that. You know he wouldn't!"

"What *did* he do?" Jase demanded grimly.

"Nothing! It's all my fault."

Her fault? The slight lifting of the dread inside him should have made him feel ashamed. Slowly he said, "So, what did *you* do?"

"I didn't exactly *do* anything," she said, "except marry him when I knew that…" She looked away. "I don't want to talk about it."

"Not even to him?"

"*Especially* not to him. It's not some tiff that can be resolved by talking."

Baffled, he said, "Well, kiddo, if you feel like drowning your sorrows, or want a shoulder to cry on, come over to my place. I've got some pretty good wine we can open." He grabbed one of her dark curls and gave it a gentle tug, then left her.

Surely this was nothing to do with Samantha? The way she'd kissed him on Saturday he'd been certain she couldn't still be in love with Bryn. Or even think she was.

And, he realised, he was also sure now that she'd never had designs on his brother-in-law. There was a lot he didn't know about her, but his gut told him she wouldn't deliberately break up a marriage. Whatever hang-ups she had, whatever feelings she might once have had for Bryn, she was honest and true and Rachel had nothing to fear from her.

The revelation lifted a weight he hadn't known he'd been carrying. *This* was what he needed to tell Samantha. That he had faith in her integrity. Before he told her anything else.

He went back up the driveway to work and spent most of the day at his desk surrounded by his staff. After they'd left he went on working, partly because he felt guilty about his lack of concentration during the day, and partly to clear some uninterrupted time to spend in Auckland, to convince Samantha that they needed to see where that kiss they'd shared might take them. That it was important for both of them.

At last he got up, made himself a hasty meal and was deep in a computer science magazine article about quantum physics when the automatic buzzer connected to the front door burred, and he saw Rachel's face on the built-in screen.

After he'd ushered her into his living room she said, "Mum and Dad are treating me like a ticking bomb. When they aren't tiptoeing around they're offering cake or coffee, or advice. I love them and I'm grateful, but…"

"Uh-huh," Jase said warily. He wasn't sure how he was supposed to treat her, but obviously being coddled wasn't it. "Want to watch TV with me?"

"Love to!" He guessed she was happy not to have to talk.

He broke out a bottle of red wine and produced the remains of the cheese he'd shared with Samantha. They drank and nibbled through a couple of programmes and then watched a film from his collection until after midnight.

He saw Rachel grow seemingly relaxed and then droopy, her legs tucked under her on the sofa, her arm resting on a cushion while she sipped at the wine.

The film over, he lifted the remote and switched off.

Rachel was swirling the last of the wine in her glass.

"You okay?" he asked.

She tried to smile, but a tear slipped down her cheek and impatiently she wiped it away. "Sorry. I've got to stop this." Her voice was muffled, a little slurred.

"Feel free. Maybe the wine was a mistake." He wondered if she'd eaten anything before arriving at his door.

"No. It helps…a bit. Just this once, though." She brushed away another tear. "My biggest mistake was marrying Bryn. His, too."

"Yeah? Why?"

She was staring down at her glass, her voice so low she might have been talking to herself. "I can't give him what he wants. Needs. If I'd known, I would never have married him. I saw him today with Samantha Magnussen. She's the kind of woman he—"

"Samantha?" Jase felt as if he'd been doused in icy water, his whole body going rigid, his chest tight.

Rachel looked up, startled. "You know her, don't you? Of course, you've been working for her, Bryn said." Her voice wobbled and she blinked hard. "She's beautiful, and clever—"

"So are you!" Jase said loyally. "And he married *you*."

"I would never have let him if I'd known…" Her lips

trembled and her voice lowered. "I've had a nasty shock." She lifted her glass and finished the wine in it, blinked again and said, "Is there any more?" holding out the glass.

"You've had enough." It seemed to be his week for getting the women in his life on the wrong side of sober. Not something he made a habit of. "If you'd known...?"

She looked as though she'd forgotten what she was talking about, her eyes tragic but unseeing. "I feel so inadequate as a woman," she whispered, her head lowered. "I did mean to talk to Bryn, when I found out... But then, seeing them together like that... Two of kind, I thought. She'd be so *right* for him."

"No." *Wrong.* "Where was this?"

"His office. I'd parked at the Donovan's building while I was in town." Rachel's eyes glazed, as if she'd blanked him out. "I did mean to talk to Bryn when I got back," she whispered. "They didn't see me. He kissed her and I was jealous. I wanted to ask him what she was doing there, with him. Stupid." A watery smile wavered on her lips. "How pathetic was that?"

Pictures ran through his head of Samantha locked in a passionate embrace with Bryn in his office, the two of them so lost in each other they didn't even notice Bryn's wife. "You had every right!"

His harsh tone wakened his sister from her reverie. "As if it mattered anyway." Almost idly she said, "Do you think they might have been lovers before?"

Jase remained silent, hoping the question was rhetorical. Hoping the past tense was the correct one.

"He admires Samantha," Rachel said mournfully. "The very first time I saw her, I could see she was attracted to him."

Just as Jase had known, the first time *he'd* seen her.

Rachel appeared to be pondering something, having

trouble concentrating. She said, "I s'pose…" she paused again "…she's got a company to run. Maybe she doesn't want marriage—or children. Bryn married me because Pearl's anxious for him to carry on the Donovan legacy, you see. And maybe partly because…well, he always liked me. I knew he didn't love me the way I love him. Only I never exsh—expected I'd fail so s-spectac-ularly—" she enunciated with great care "—at the thing that really mattered."

Sex? Jase assumed. He had a hunch Rachel hadn't known much about it, bar the theory, but surely Bryn could have—

He didn't want to know about that. Not between his sister and…anybody.

Rachel's eyes were bleak now but dry. "So I did the only thing I could."

Rage almost boiled over in Jase. He'd always known his sister was cuckoo over Bryn, but she was a fighter by nature. Seeing her fold this way was unnervingly out of character. He supposed pride would have stopped her from sticking around, no matter how much she loved her husband.

"You're right, I've had too much to drink. And talked too much." She yawned, and muttered, "I should go home. I mean back to…"

Carefully she put down her glass and made to get up, only to fall back against the cushions. "Soon," she said, her eyelids falling closed.

Jase got up, lifted her feet onto the sofa and adjusted the cushions behind her head. She murmured something unintelligible; then her breathing slowed and deepened. He fetched a light coverlet, tucked it around her, and went to bed himself. His parents would know she was safe with him.

* * *

Samantha had been in her office for only minutes when she heard Jase's voice, and moments later her door was flung open. She caught a glimpse of her secretary behind him, astonished and worried. The look on Jase's face made her own heart lurch and she automatically stood up as he entered like a force of nature.

"Tell your secretary you don't want to be disturbed," he said. "This is private and personal."

It took Samantha a moment to gather her wits and make a quick decision. She nodded at Judy across his shoulder, saying, "I'll call if I need you."

Jase slammed the door, his face the personification of a thundercloud.

"What is this about?" she demanded, getting in first. "I'm not in the habit of taking orders from other people about my staff. If you have business with me—"

"You can just climb down off that high and mighty perch of yours, *ice lady*! I said this is personal."

He hadn't called her "ice lady" or "ice princess" for a long time. Unexpectedly it hurt. Her facial muscles stiffened, and she knew she was living up to the epithet. "If you think my spending a few hours with you and your family gives you any right to barge in here and—"

"And what gives you the right to go around kissing married men? And more, I suppose, than kissing!"

Taking a moment to process his obvious misconception, she said, keeping her voice calm and steadying it with an effort, "If you mean Bryn, I haven't kissed him since his wedding. And that was just a friendly peck."

"Don't lie to me!" He came closer, splaying his hands on her desk. "You nearly had me fooled last weekend, but—"

"I'm not lying!" She was glad the desk was between them. He looked about ready to do her serious bodily harm.

But Samantha Magnussen had never given in to bullying. She leaned towards him, bringing her face within a handspan of his glittering eyes. Her voice now at freezing level, she said, "You can stop yelling at me, and get out of my office until you calm down."

"So make me!" he invited, not flinching away from her deliberately chilling gaze.

Samantha made to pick up her desk phone, but faster than lightning he grabbed her wrist, simultaneously moving round the desk and pulling her to him.

She had barely opened her mouth to call out in alarm before his fingers twisted into her hair, tipping her head back, and then his mouth was on hers.

It was less a kiss than an assault, aimed only at shutting her up. She squirmed against the iron-hard clasp of his arm about her waist, lifted her hands to tug at his hair, and when he merely tightened his grip on hers, she tried to scratch at his face. He captured her hand and clipped it behind her back, then grabbed the other too and held both her wrists there, in one of his hands.

She wrenched her head aside, freeing her mouth, but it would be too embarrassing to be found like this if she called for help. Samantha fought her own battles.

She tried to say, "What do you—" *think you're doing?*

He cut her off, grasping her chin so she had to face him again. "If you want a man," he rasped, his eyes aflame with temper, "choose one that's available. Like me."

CHAPTER NINE

THEN he was kissing her again—passionate and long and slow, sexy enough to make her toes curl, to flood her with melting heat.

Not that she'd allow him to know that. With a supreme act of will she stayed stiff and unresponsive in his arms, counting to fifty, making herself open her eyes, trying to stare at a wall, the ceiling, anything but him.

It only made her eyes water, and she had to close them in the end. His tongue darted into her mouth, withdrawing again when she tried to bite. The pressure on her lips eased as she felt him silently laugh. He closed his teeth gently about her lower lip for an instant, sending a bolt of liquid heat through her. Then he drew away and released her hands.

Without even thinking she swung at him, delivering a ringing slap on his cheek that jerked his head to one side.

"Wow!" he said without touching his face. "You pack a punch, ice lady." But in a millisecond he was smiling at her grimly. "I always suspected there was fire underneath there somewhere. Bring it on, sweetheart, but it'd be more fun in bed."

Despite the so-called smile she knew he was still deep-down, frighteningly angry. So was she, although trembling inside with myriad conflicting emotions. "Get out of my office—my building!" she said, almost choking on her own anger, compounded by a crashing disappointment. "And if you set foot in it again I'll have Security throw you out."

Jase shoved his hands into his pockets, and she had the distinct impression it was to keep himself from grabbing her again—to kiss or kill she didn't know.

"Suits me," he said. "You'll be thrilled to know you've ruined my sister's life. Next time I see you it'll be in hell, if I have anything to do with it."

He was out the door before she'd processed that, leaving her staring at the blank panel.

The phone on her desk buzzed, then buzzed again. She picked it up and her secretary asked, "Um, is everything all right?"

Everything was a total mess. And Samantha had no idea why. She took a moment to steady her voice, and into the silence Judy said, "I've never seen Mr Moore—look like that."

"Oh, you know these creative types," Samantha said lightly. "I'm sure we can fix the problem. Give me ten minutes to finish what I'm doing here, and then can you bring in a printout of the figures for the Harvey project?" It was the first thing that caught her eye on the day's to-do list sitting in front of her. It would keep Judy out of here while she rallied herself.

She sat down in her chair, her legs still shaking, and stared at the wall until her secretary tapped on the door, giving her a concerned look as she handed over the requested file.

Snap out of it, she told herself, taking the file. "Thanks, Judy," she said dismissively, and opened it up, pretending to study the first page until she heard the door close again. The print blurred before her eyes and she closed them tightly, counted slowly to a hundred, and with a brutal effort made herself focus on business.

Jase knew he should have calmed down before leaving his sister back at his parents' house and driving straight to Auckland and Samantha's office, but after a sleepless night following Rachel's revelations he'd been progressively more and more enraged.

He'd heard Rachel in the shower and had juice, toast and coffee ready for her in the kitchen when she emerged in her rumpled clothing, and he made her sit down with him and eat, though she only nibbled at some toast spread with Vegemite, and drank three cups of coffee.

"What you said last night, about Bryn and—" he started, but didn't get a chance to finish.

The mention of her husband's name seemed to produce panic, her eyes wide and fixed on his. "Don't tell anyone!" she said. "I know I rambled on about...well, things. All that wine. I probably didn't make any sense. But you're not to repeat any of it to *anyone*, you hear?"

"If it's true he—"

"Of course it's true, but no one else has to know. It's too humiliating—and whatever I told you, it stays between you and me, understand?"

Jase scowled. "Sounds to me like your husband needs a bit of a shake-up. I've a good mind—"

"Don't you dare!" She glared at him. "If you breathe a word to him I'll never forgive you, I swear. If you even *think* about it!"

She'd made him promise not to talk to Bryn or their parents, so worked up he reluctantly gave in.

As to not thinking about it, that wasn't so easy.

Hours after the fiasco in Samantha's office he was still thinking about it, sitting in his own Auckland office and supposedly working on a quote for a new client. Although Rachel's ban hadn't specifically included Samantha, she wouldn't in any way approve his crashing in to accuse her, telling her she'd ruined his sister's life. And certainly not of his kissing the woman who'd wrecked Rachel's marriage.

But that was between him and Samantha. Because...well, because she'd almost had him convinced he was wrong. That she was no marriage-wrecker, that there was a chance—

His thought processes came to a crashing halt.

A chance for them. For him and Samantha. Protecting his sister's marriage? A smokescreen, a cover for what he really wanted—*Samantha*. In his bed, in his life.

Someone tapped on the door and came in—his sales manager.

"Yes?" Jase snarled, thrusting the troubling idea from his mind. "What?"

The young man took a step back. "If this is a bad time—"

"No." Jase forced a smile. He'd always run his business on the basis of being readily available to his staff. "I need a distraction." And wasn't that the truth? "Sit down and tell me what's up."

Four times that day Samantha picked up her phone to call Jase, and each time put it down again. She had a right to an explanation of his extraordinary behaviour that morning. To demand it from him.

On the other hand, why should she be the one to make the first move? She'd done nothing to deserve that tirade. She debated calling Bryn, find out what was going on, but when she finally phoned his office she was told he wasn't in that day. She could try Rivermeadows, she supposed, ask Lady Pearl if something was wrong, but then she'd have to explain why she was asking. And she had no intention of describing Jase's visit.

There must be a misunderstanding—maybe Bryn and Rachel had some domestic differences. None of her business, and none of Jase's either. She tried to stir up righteous anger but it didn't dispel the hollow despair that was much stronger. Probably Jase didn't know what had gone wrong, just that something had, and simply jumped to a totally irrational conclusion that it was her fault because he'd never got over his first hasty judgement of her.

It would all blow over and Jase would come crawling back to apologise. Except she didn't think he'd ever crawl to anyone. He was too damned self-righteous and arrogant for that.

She'd thought he'd put his distrust of her behind them, that they had established at least a reasonable working relationship, had even contemplated an affair. When he'd kissed her at his home she'd been on the verge of something she'd never experienced. Of losing herself in another person—a man.

All day she felt as if a lead balloon was lodged in her chest, ever-expanding and threatening to burst out in a storm of tears. She gritted her teeth and reminded herself there were things to be done, people to see, important matters to attend to. A business to run. It had always saved her before in her down times. She had never allowed petty personal problems to distract her.

And she wouldn't now.

For a whole week, despite her determination to put him out of her mind, Samantha was on tenterhooks, expecting to hear

DAPHNE CLAIR   129

from a contrite and chastened Jase, but there was nothing. She considered confronting Rachel and demanding to know why Jase thought Samantha had ruined her life. But making anyone else aware of her very private pain—the thought made her shrivel inside.

The days dragged, and the longer the silence continued the harder it became for her to pick up the phone and call him.

It hurt that he'd misjudged her, hurt that he'd been so ready to blame her, but his absence hurt the most—more than she'd ever thought possible.

There came a day when she could bear it no longer. She phoned his Auckland office and in a businesslike tone asked to speak to him, only to be told he was out of the country on a big overseas project, and not expected back for several weeks. Could a staff member help? Or she could get in touch by e-mail if she liked. He'd be collecting his mail regularly and—

"No, thanks," she said. "It can wait."

She put down the receiver, feeling oddly blank. So that was that. Chasing him down wherever he was in the world was too much for her self-respect to take.

Something stung at the back of her eyes. She'd been working too hard. She needed...a walk on the beach came to mind, and she recalled the day Jase had taken her to the wild west coast and they'd strolled side by side barefoot on the sand; remembered his strong hand steadying her as they climbed the rocks—and the moment when she'd fallen practically into his arms.

The day he'd taken her to his home, when it seemed he might even be coming to like her—she'd thought he wasn't just lusting for her against his will. Thought that something might come of the attraction that had arced and pulsed between them from that first, thorny meeting. Something vital, tender and trusting.

When they'd kissed that night it had seemed right, a step into unknown but welcoming territory with a man different from every other man she'd known. A man who was open and sometimes brutally frank, but was always honest. Not afraid to say what he thought, show what he felt. Her opposite in fact, and maybe that was why she'd fallen in—

She sat stunned. She'd fallen in love with Jase Moore. Against all odds, all reason, he'd stormed her heart and made off with it. She wanted him as she'd never in her life wanted anything. Not her father's respect, not her mother's approval. She wanted Jase so badly her body shook and her heart hammered, longing flooding her entire body and mind.

And he didn't want her. Not the way she'd hoped—had thought he might one day. The passion in his kiss might have expressed the craving of his body, but the angry contempt in it had dashed any hope of tenderness—of love.

At the next board meeting, she was shocked at Bryn's appearance—the new prominence of his strong cheekbones, his hollowed eyes. There was no chance to talk with him alone, and he left as soon as the meeting finished.

She made an excuse to see him the following day, citing a minor problem that had been discussed without resolution at the meeting, and suggested they meet for lunch at a restaurant they'd used often in the past, before his marriage. Since then she'd been wary of such tête à têtes.

He hesitated before agreeing, and when he entered the place where she was waiting for him, he still had that grim and haunted look.

Business was soon dispensed with and, trying to sound casual, she asked, "How is Rachel?"

"Fine," he answered shortly, digging his fork into a bowl of pasta, and repeating the action twice before he looked up, shocking her again with the bleakness of his gaze.

He dropped the fork, ran a hand over his dark hair and muttered, "Oh, what the hell. The truth is I have no idea. Happy, I suppose." He sat tense and frowning. "It'll be common knowledge soon. She's left me, Sam."

Samantha pushed aside her smoked kingfish. "Permanently?"

He lifted a shoulder. "She was very clear about that. Yes." He was trying to sound blasé, but she knew him well enough to recognise it for an act. The man was suffering.

"I'm so sorry, Bryn." And she was indignant on his behalf. "Are you sure there's no chance of—"

"She's in love with someone else," he said baldly. His fingers curled about the stem of his wineglass but he just twirled it broodingly instead of lifting it to drink.

Was the woman mad? Even though Samantha no longer yearned after Bryn, she still thought Rachel was one of the luckiest women in the world. She sat in speechless, stunned sympathy.

The flatness of his tone heart-rending, he said, "She said she's found her true love. I should be glad for her but—"

Impulsively she placed a hand over his, surprised when in a reflex action he opened his fist and clung as if to a lifeline. Looking down, he said, "Sorry, Sam. Inflicting my troubles on you."

"We're friends. Anything I can do…"

"Thanks. But there's nothing." He stared down at their hands for a time in silence, apparently deriving some comfort from her sympathy. When he released his grip her fingers ached but she didn't complain.

She thought of telling him about Jase's bizarre suspicions, but it wouldn't help either of them, might even embarrass Bryn and sour their friendship.

Neither of them finished their meal. When they parted outside the restaurant Bryn kissed her cheek, and with her heart aching for him she gave him a warm, comforting hug before he went striding off along the street.

If Rachel had left him for someone else, why had Jase thought Samantha was to blame?

Even though she kept in touch with Bryn, she wasn't aware that Jase was back in the country until she attended the annual Donovan's Charity Ball, an event she'd missed only once since returning from Australia.

What she had not expected was that Jase would be there too. Somehow she'd assumed that since Rachel's defection Bryn's ties with her family would have been severed. But of course he would still have a business relationship with Jase's company. All Donovan's business contacts would have been invited.

Seeing him chatting with a group of people at one of the circular tables she wondered if the very attractive young woman next to him was his partner this evening. When he looked up as if he'd felt her staring, she hastily averted her eyes and led the man she'd brought along towards a table where some people she knew were already seated. She'd have preferred to have her back to the one where Jase was, but the chair her escort pulled out for her had a clear view of the forceful, unforgettable features she'd been trying to erase from her memory.

He was looking straight back at her, in the same hostile, accusing way he had the very first time she'd seen him. She turned to the man still standing behind her chair, raising her face to him as he bent to ask, "Can I get you something to drink?"

She asked for sparkling wine, and chatted to the other people at the table until he returned and seated himself at her side, hooking an arm companionably across the back of her chair. Samantha was glad she had invited him. He was a widower, a nice middle-aged furniture company director who was wary of relationships after the abrupt end to his happy marriage. He and his wife had both been keen dancers and he missed that a lot, he'd told Samantha. They found each other useful on occasions such as this.

She was glad too that she'd worn a dress she'd fallen in love with—a blue silk only slightly darker than her eyes, with a faux 1930s elegance relying on cut rather than embellishment. With it she wore a pair of glittering pale blue topaz teardrop earrings and a silver bracelet set with the same stones.

She sipped at her champagne, her face set in a pleasantly smooth social mask, exchanging platitudes until one of the women said, "Where's Bryn's lovely wife? I don't see her here."

"They've separated," another woman told her. "Didn't you know? There was a piece in that gossip column of Cynthia's a while ago. Rachel seems to have disappeared from view." Turning to Samantha, she added, "You know him pretty well, don't you? Any idea what happened?"

Samantha shrugged. "Bryn and I are business friends. His personal life is his own affair." Then she changed the subject to the charity auction that traditionally formed part of the entertainment, the night's proceeds going to help sick children. She'd donated a piece of her mother's jewellery—a heavy diamond-and-wrought-silver necklace that she'd never particularly liked.

Samantha and her widower friend had taken to the floor several times before Bryn arrived at their table and asked her to dance with him, saying, "I've done all my duty dances."

She thought about Jase balefully watching them, and deliberately pushed him out of her mind as she rose and followed him.

There were still signs of strain around his eyes, in the set of his mouth. When Jase passed them, his arm around the pretty girl he'd been sitting next to, she quickly averted her gaze. It was the first time this evening they'd been near each other, although he'd been dancing with the girl earlier, and once she saw him with an older woman.

Bryn returned her to her seat and lingered for a few minutes talking to the others round the table. Then she and her partner went to view the items for auction later. Her mother's necklace was displayed on a table among other jewellery and antique ornaments. On the floor stood things like brand-new water pumps and garden gadgets, office machines and household whiteware.

Samantha's companion became absorbed in inspecting a large and gleaming bright-red ride-on mower. He climbed onto the seat and began fiddling with levers, and she smilingly left him to it and moved on, attracted by a set of silk cushions embroidered and beaded in gold and jewel colours. Perhaps they'd add warmth and a touch of the exotic to her living room, which she had lately found rather stark.

Stepping away, she cannoned into a solid shape behind her and turned to apologise, half expecting to see one of the burly security guards who were watching over the display.

What she saw was Jase, so close she could smell the fabric of his evening shirt, and a hint of soap.

She felt his hand on her arm like a manacle before he dropped it and she backed against the table, the apology dying on her lips.

They were hemmed in amongst other people, and he seemed transfixed, as she was, both of them simply staring at each other for what seemed like an age, though it could only have been seconds at most.

"Samantha," he said at last. And then, his voice barely audible among the increasingly loud chatter all about them, "Who's the guy with you? A smokescreen? Why bother, now you've got what you wanted? Or isn't it working out after all? Bryn looks to me like he's not too happy with his life. Is his conscience bothering him, or have you had a falling out?"

"Why don't you ask him?" Samantha hissed, unspeakably hurt. She'd still had some vague hope that Jase would have realised how wrong he was, would admit it and apologise. But since returning to New Zealand he'd come nowhere near her. He still hated her.

Had he all along? It struck her, sickeningly, that his apparent thawing, the walk on the beach, the almost-friendship during his makeover of her company's systems, the visit to his parents and his home—even the kiss—might have been part of a calculated plan to keep her away from Bryn, distract her by offering himself instead. It was what he'd said to her in her office, raging, *If you want a man, choose one who's free. Like me.*

But then he'd kissed her. He had still wanted her in that way—even if he hated her. Her angry, ignoble triumph at that was no compensation for him not even liking her. But it helped to hide the hurt.

He said, "I did ask Bryn what the hell was going on with you two. He decked me."

She blinked. Bryn was the most self-controlled person she knew. Not that Jase didn't deserve it. "Didn't that give you a clue?" she asked incredulously.

Someone jostled her, a woman saying irritably, "Excuse me, I just want to look at—"

Samantha missed hearing the rest. Jase had taken hold of her arm again and was hauling her after him, pushing through the throng until they emerged in a clear space and he found an empty corner half screened by a palm in a huge pot that blocked any escape. He growled, "Sure it gave me a clue. He wouldn't tell me a damn thing. Which seems to me like a guilty conscience."

"He has nothing to feel guilty about!" Samantha protested.

Jase exploded. "What the hell is it about the guy and you women, that you all stick up for him? Even Rachel—"

"Because he hasn't *done* anything!" Samantha said. "It was *Rachel* who left *him*."

"I know that. And I know why."

He did? And still he blamed Bryn—and her? It didn't compute. "Bryn told you?" she asked.

"Rachel told me. She saw you two together."

"What do you mean, together? You know we—"

"Kissing," he said harshly. "Making love at Bryn's office. You didn't even know she was there."

For once she was unable to control her expression. Her eyes widened and her lips parted in silent protest. Her voice wavered. "She's lying!" *Why?* To conceal her own infidelity from her brother, the rest of her family?

His eyes narrowed. "My sister doesn't lie."

Stuttering with shock, she said, "We—we've—hardly even touched when we've been in Bryn's office." Belatedly she added, "Or anywhere. It's not true!"

This couldn't really be happening, could it? "Jase—" she reached out a hand to touch him, her fingers on the sleeve of his jacket, her voice still unsteady "—*it isn't true.*"

For a couple of seconds he stared at her, and doubt flickered in his eyes. Then they hardened and he shook off her hand as though it were an annoying insect. "She wouldn't say so if it wasn't true. And she's not the only one."

Samantha recoiled. *"What?"*

"You haven't heard the talk?"

She should have realised that people would jump to conclusions, seeing her and Bryn together more often in the wake of his marriage breakup. They were both high-profile businesspeople, marks for public speculation. "Anonymous gossip is hardly a reliable—"

"Not all of it's anonymous," he interrupted harshly. "A friend, with no reason to make it up. She saw you holding hands with Bryn in a restaurant downtown. Staring into each other's eyes as if you'd forgotten anyone else was there, embracing right outside the doorway where everyone could see. If you two can't keep your hands to yourselves in public, why the pretence tonight?"

"There's no pretence!" This had gone too far. "Jase, you don't underst—"

"A lovers' quarrel then?" he asked, shoving a hand into the pocket of his trousers, his lip curling. "You trying to make him jealous?"

She opened her mouth to reply, but another male figure appeared behind Jase. "Samantha?" Her partner of the evening, having finally abandoned his love affair with the lawnmower. "Everything all right?"

Jase didn't even look at him, his eyes raking Samantha with a hostile, deliberately insulting glance that made her heart shrivel. "She's all yours, mate," he tossed contemptuously in the direction of the other man, and strode away.

"Who's he?" Her partner frowned. "Are you okay?"

"Someone I've done business with in the past," she said carefully. "And of course I'm okay." She tried a smile, hoping he couldn't see she was shaking inside. "Have you decided to bid for the mower?"

"Maybe." Apparently not convinced of her disclaimer, he put an arm about her as he led her back to their table. By the time they reached it she had regained her composure and was able to pretend nothing had happened.

The floor was cleared for the auction and the necklace fetched a good price. Her mother would have been pleased. One of her favourite charities had been the children's hospital. It was probably selfish of Samantha to wish her mother had spent less time sitting on committees for good causes, or "making contacts" at bridge parties and fashion shows, and more with her only child.

She'd been someone who needed other people around, restless and bored when her only companion was a little girl. Samantha had tried to grow up fast, to copy her pretty, popular, socialite mother—while at the same time trying to become her father's worthy successor. It had been a difficult balancing act.

When the cushions Samantha had admired came up for sale she put in a bid but her heart wasn't in it, and when another bidder seemed set on acquiring them she dropped out. Later she entered a bid for a lovely octagonal parquet occasional table on low splayed legs trimmed with brass. She wanted to contribute to the cause and the piece seemed about to go for much less than it was worth. Eventually it was knocked down to her and she wondered how it would fit into her décor. Perhaps she'd use it to hold a vase of flowers.

After the auction the music became livelier and the

younger contingent dominated the floor. She saw Jase with the girl who might be his partner for the night—and more? He was just as good at the hip-swivelling, foot-stomping style as he was at traditional dance steps.

The night dragged on, and around midnight Samantha asked her escort to take her home, suddenly deathly tired and with an incipient headache. They took a taxi, and when they reached her home he got the cab to wait while he walked her to her door, refusing to let her pay her share of the fare. "Don't be silly," he said. "You bought the tickets and I had a very nice time. I enjoyed the dancing. Thank you." He touched his lips to her cheek, and left.

There were nice people in the world, she thought, closing the door and switching on the hall light. A pity she couldn't have fallen for one of them, instead of a man who was too ready to believe the worst of her. And who might have been playing with her emotions.

Once in her bed, she stared into the darkness for a while before closing her eyes. All she could see was Jase, his face dark with fury, his eyes filled with contempt and dislike. And all she could feel was hurt and anger and desolation.

No matter what she said he wouldn't believe her. He believed the preposterous story Rachel had apparently told him.

Why would Rachel have made up something like that? And how dare she implicate Samantha?

The pieces of the puzzle didn't fit.

CHAPTER TEN

JASE didn't remember a time when he'd been reluctant to go to work. Or felt that having his home and his office in the same building was a mistake.

His staff were at their desks below while he still sat slumped over the remains of his breakfast, the cereal hardening at the edges of the bowl he'd shoved away, and toast crumbs sticking to a plate while his third cup of coffee cooled between his hands.

Since he was a night owl by nature, it wasn't unusual for him to be at his computer into the early hours solving a particularly sticky problem, or to leave his bed because in the half-conscious state between the real world and sleep a new idea had filtered into his brain, and he needed to get it on the screen where he could see if it had any substance or was merely a crazy dream.

Crazy dreams had sometimes led to new, groundbreaking realities. And after years of working on his own he found it stimulating being among others with the same eagerness to make the impossible possible.

The last few nights he'd been sleepless yet unable to work. Even when he turned on his computer and stared at the screen nothing came. And in the daytime he hadn't wanted to face his colleagues, wanting only to be alone to brood.

All because of seeing Samantha again at the Donovan's Charity Ball, so serene and beautiful and untouchable, and after one brief, indifferent glance ignoring him.

Not unexpected, considering their last encounter, but it had ignited a slow-smouldering rage that he couldn't shake. He'd had to summon all his willpower to keep up an appearance of enjoying himself so as not to spoil the party for the wife and daughter of his sales director, who had persuaded him that the networking opportunity was too valuable to turn down.

The two women, particularly the daughter, were excited at being his guests at the Donovan's Ball. While the sales director worked the room, Jase had done his best to entertain them, feeling old and jaded at the girl's awed enthusiasm. She was a nice kid, and he'd made sure she had a night to remember—for all the right reasons. He suspected he wasn't going to forget it for a long time either, but for all the wrong reasons. Like the fact he hadn't been able to resist baiting Samantha when they literally bumped into each other.

For once she couldn't quite hide her emotions, looking shocked when he confronted her with the evidence. And as guilty as hell for a second or two before she accused Rachel of lying.

He knew his sister better than that. And anyway, what reason would she have?

What he didn't understand was why Samantha didn't just admit that she and Bryn were having an affair, or were at least close to it. Probably picking up where they'd left off before. Rachel had seemed to think that likely.

The hell of it was, he admitted silently as he dumped cold

coffee in the sink and added his breakfast dishes to the others already in the dishwasher, that no matter what he told himself about Samantha's deceit and her cold-hearted treatment of his sister, he couldn't stop wanting her.

An overnight electrical storm hit Auckland, knocking out phones, fax machines and computers all over the city. Despite the safeguards Jase's team had installed, a direct lightning strike on the roof of the Magnussen Building affected some of the company's network. The IT manager called and demanded action.

Samantha reassured herself that it wouldn't be likely that Jase himself would be needed, but after a couple of technicians had worked on the problems all morning and then left, saying everything tested okay now, half an hour later her secretary informed her he was on the line.

Tempted to tell Judy to say she was out to lunch, Samantha decided that would be cowardly and took the call, annoyed to find her palm on the receiver was moist. She said crisply, "Yes?"

"Just checking," he said, "that you're happy—"

"*What?*" Had he phoned to harass her again about her supposed affair with Bryn?

"—with the job my team did on your computers," he said. "I'm making sure all my clients are satisfied."

Samantha closed her eyes and bit her lip, glad he couldn't see her. One thing she'd been adamant about *not* wanting was a phone-camera link. "You're ringing them all personally?"

"That's right. It's business, Samantha." His voice was as smooth as butter.

She covered the mouthpiece and took a deep breath before

removing her hand. "Yes, well—they seem to have done a good job. No one's complained so far."

"If they do, get your IT guy to give me a call."

"Thank you, I'll do that."

There was a hiatus, and she clutched the phone, reluctant to put it down.

Then he said, "Fine. See you."

She heard the click of the receiver, and knew that despite the last statement he didn't intend to see her at all. He often ended calls with that casual, meaningless goodbye. Even shop assistants she'd never seen before and probably never would again sometimes used it instead of the equally hollow, "Have a good day."

She replaced the receiver, her throat tight and aching, her eyes stinging, and in her mind repeated a mantra, *I never cry, I am not crying, I will not cry, I never...*

She pulled opened her drawer to haul a tissue out of its box, intending to wipe her hands, but it brought a wad of others with it. Stuffing them back in, she swore softly but vigorously, then scrubbed at her damp palms and swiped away a single escaping tear, sniffed, and wiped her nose too before throwing the tissue into the bin.

At least swearing was better than weeping. It had worked for her father, hadn't it? Although he had made clear his disapproval of his daughter doing the same.

Her mother had used tears as a tool to get what she wanted. Something Samantha had made up her mind not to do. She'd accept a kiss on the cheek instead of a handshake from a male colleague, give a congratulatory touch instead of a backslap, deliver a pat or briefly stroke his arm for commiseration— even hug him if she knew him well.

And she wasn't above using her eyes, her smile, to win a man over to her viewpoint if it was important enough. Particularly if he was the patronising type who responded better to feminine charm than to simple, obvious evidence that she could do her job as well as any man.

In a business where sexism was still subtly and sometimes glaringly present, she'd use any weapon she could call to hand. Except the ultimate female one.

For the rest of the day she worked as usual, but without being able to shake the sound of Jase's voice from some secret inner ear. As they had for days, the same questions came back to haunt her.

Halfway through the afternoon she made a phone call to Bryn, on the excuse of asking him if Donovan's had suffered any damage from the storm.

"Very little," he replied. "Jase sent someone in to check our systems, and found a few minor problems."

"Did he phone you to check later?"

"Yes. He runs a good service. Are you okay over there?"

"Fine." So Jase's claim to be checking on his clients was true. He wasn't driven by some need to speak to her.

She hesitated then. If she were a smoker, she thought irrelevantly, a cigarette might have made this easier—a long, slow hit of nicotine. But she'd always been chary of addictions—of anything with the potential to take over her body or her mind.

And what good had that done her once Jase Moore sailed into her life? She couldn't even get through the day without him affecting both.

Bryn said, "Is there something you want, Samantha?"

She breathed in and out. "You know there are rumours going round—about you and me?"

After a second he said, "My policy has always been to ignore cheap gossip. I hope it isn't going to affect our friendship."

"No! It's just that…Jase thinks there's something in it." Her voice had sunk to almost a whisper.

"Jase?" And then he said slowly, "So that's what it was about!"

The confrontation when Bryn had punched Jase, presumably. "Rachel told him she saw us," Samantha explained. "You and me…t-together."

"So what? We've often been toge—" He broke off. She heard him draw a breath. "She can't have told him that. Her leaving had nothing to do with you. I'll straighten Jase out if you like." His voice suddenly sharp and curious, he asked, "Is it important to you?"

"No," she said quickly. "Don't do that." Leaving the ambiguity in the air. Having Bryn fight her battles wasn't an option. "He told me at the Donovan's ball that you hit him."

Bryn sounded rueful. "I guess because of course I couldn't hit Rachel. I was feeling pretty raw and angry. I'm damned sure she didn't ask him to interfere."

"You didn't tell him…"

"No. If she hadn't told him that she'd found someone else, it wasn't up to me. You and my mother are the only ones who know. And I did apologise for the punch."

And she supposed, manlike, they rubbed along together now. For women, conflict was less simply resolved with an outburst of physical aggression.

He said, "Jase has always been close to Rachel. When they were kids he even had a go at Ben if he teased her. He's a good guy, Sam, if a bit overprotective."

He was tiptoeing round the subject of her relationship with Jase.

She might have told him there wasn't one, that even if there had been a slight possibility it had withered on the vine, succumbing to the worm of distrust and the blight of disbelief.

That evening after the storm had passed, leaving only occasional drizzle behind, she was watching a film on TV, trying to blank her mind to all else, and had just pressed the remote at the third lot of ads when her doorbell pealed.

Assuming it was one of the neighbours, perhaps the retired accountant next door who was a keen fisherman and sometimes dropped off a fresh kahawai or snapper for her, she unlocked the door and opened it, stepping back quickly as Jase pushed it wider and strode into the small entryway. His hair was more unruly than usual, and she had trouble reading his expression. Fed up? Angry? Obstinate?

He said, "Don't tell me to go away. Where can we talk?" He saw the open doorway to the lounge, where the TV and one of the sofas was visible, clasped her arm and drew her into the room.

"Why are you here?" she asked, trying to smother a glimmer of hope fighting through the resentment that had closed about her heart.

He searched her eyes with a gimletlike gaze, then made an impatient sound. "Are you going to ask me to sit down? Do you want to finish watching your programme?"

"No," she said. "I mean, sit down if you like." She walked over to switch off the set.

When she turned he was ensconcing himself in a chair. He wore jeans and a black crew-neck shirt and smelled of rain. The shirt was darkened on the shoulders and there were tiny droplets in his hair. The storm had blown southward but the wind had gusted all day, with intermittent misty showers. She wondered how long he'd been out in the rain.

She said, "Can I get you a drink? Or coffee?" She could do with a strong one herself, but it probably would be a mistake.

Jase shook his head. "I just had coffee. Lots of it."

She sat opposite him, upright and with her hands folded in her lap, as she'd been taught as a little girl to sit when there were visitors. "What can I do for you?" she asked.

His lips twitched and he drawled, "Now there's an interesting question."

"If you've come here to make suggestive adolescent remarks—" Her temper was slipping a little, and she made an effort to keep it leashed.

"No," he said, holding up a hand then lowering it. He looked at her intently, as if trying to fathom her thoughts. "I came to—" he ran a hand over his hair, which did almost nothing to smooth it "—have a go at sorting things out."

Hope flared again, and she quickly doused it. He might not mean what she thought. "Things?" she said cautiously. "Like what?"

His mouth thinned impatiently for a moment. "I keep telling myself it's no use, but I can't get you out of my system. I still want you, Samantha, always have. And I can't shake this crazy, irrational feeling I always will. Everything else is irrelevant. Is it the same for you?"

Samantha was speechless. Trust him to go directly to the point of his visit, dispense with any sort of finesse. One part of her was responding with a soft, sweet yearning, disarmed by his frankness. That was the emotional part. All the female areas of her body were quiveringly alert with a totally physical answer to the sexual demand in his eyes that was even more explicit than his words. And yet her mind was screaming warnings.

She had never wanted a man so much in her life. And it scared her witless.

"Well?" Jase stood up so quickly she flinched.

"I…" She paused to catch her breath, stop herself saying something inane like, *Mr Moore, this is such a surprise!*

"I'm not going to attack you!" he said, shoving his hands into the pockets of his jeans. "Were you really as cool as a bloody iceberg when I phoned today? Or were your palms sweating?"

He noticed her almost imperceptible start, and his eyes narrowed, glittering. His voice lowered. "Did you remember that kiss at my window? At that moment you were mine if only I'd been short enough of common decency to take advantage of it. You have no idea how often I lie awake wishing I had fewer principles," he told her with grim irony.

So did she, but she wasn't going to confess to that.

He said, his expression turning brooding, "When you heard my voice today, did you wish you'd come to my bed and we'd made love, with the stars overhead and the night breeze to cool the heat we shared? The heat we'd create when we touched each other, kissed each other, found out what it was like to be together, to have me inside you?"

Samantha couldn't stop the flush rising in her cheeks, spreading throughout her entire body. "No," she said. She knew he was telling her his own fantasy, and the erotic picture he drew made her pulse throb, her breasts tingle and peak.

"Samantha." He took a step and leaned over her, one hand on the arm of the sofa, the other lifting her chin so that she had to either look into his mesmerising, deep-sea eyes or close her own—which would invite…

He said very softly, "Don't lie to me. I might be wrong about a lot of things, but not about this. Nothing else matters. Whatever Rachel saw, I don't give a damn. Whoever else you've slept with in the past, you want *me* now. It's in your eyes. And—" his hand swept down the curve of her throat, over her breast, his own eyes blazing with dangerous fire "—this doesn't lie."

He didn't love her and he hadn't said anything about believing in her, only that he wanted to have sex with her—even if he did call it making love. He wasn't even pretending he had more in mind than one night. She should be grateful for his honesty.

While her body was screaming at her to take what he offered while she had the chance, the tiny rational part of her mind that was left whispered, *Save yourself.*

With a valiant effort, she said, "We can't...I *won't* go to bed with you because of an inconvenient biological reaction."

For a moment he didn't move at all, just stared into her defiant eyes while a couple of lines gradually appeared between his.

Then to her chagrined amazement his mouth widened into an unholy grin, and he began to laugh.

Samantha stood up uncertainly, seething. She said, "I'm glad I amuse you so much."

He sobered. "I'm not laughing at you, Samantha. Well, I suppose I am. It's just that 'an inconvenient biological reaction' is ludicrously inadequate for the way I feel about you."

He was trying to look sorry, although laughter still lurked in his eyes. Not derisive or cynical laughter. But inclusive, almost affectionate—inviting her to see the funny side too.

She felt her own lips reluctantly curve in response. "I suppose," she said, "it sounded rather pompous."

"It sounded like you," he said. He cocked his head to one side, examining her as if she were one of his computer problems that needed solving. "Pulling up the drawbridge and retreating to the castle keep, locking yourself away from the enemy at the gate."

She felt the tug of his attraction as though it were a physical thing, drawing her to him. "Are you my enemy?" she half-whispered, acutely aware they were standing within touching distance, that one step would bring them together. One irrevocable step.

And aware too of the danger he represented. To her integrity, her self-control, her tightly guarded heart.

But already he'd breached the walls, sent her defences tumbling—captured that heart, which she'd tried so hard to keep inviolable. It was his to treasure or trample.

"I won't hurt you," he said.

An easy promise to make. Maybe he even believed it—believed she could give her body without engaging her emotions. If he still thought she was an ice princess it was her own fault—she'd tried her best to hide her inner self from him.

She said, "You don't trust me."

"Do you trust me?"

She'd wondered if he had some Machiavellian plan to make her want him in order to save his sister's marriage. Yet everything she knew of him said he wasn't capable of duplicity. His methods were direct, his style a full-scale charge with a battering ram rather than a secretive tunnelling under the castle wall.

True to form, he hadn't tried to deceive her, had not denied that he still mistrusted her. That hurt like a poisoned dart. The initial sting, she knew, would be followed by a slowly spreading pain. But right now all other feeling was drowned out by the insistent clamour of the aching need that consumed her. If she trusted him with her body, would he come to trust her integrity in return?

Impatient with her hesitation, Jase said, "What does it matter? I don't give a damn any more about Bryn and Rachel and what she might have seen or not, the whole damned mess. Right now all that matters is this."

He reached out and took her hand, drawing her towards him, and she didn't resist. His arms went around her and her body said, *Yes!* Just this once she would allow instinct to take over, regardless of the consequences.

She saw the flare of triumph in his eyes, saw his beautiful male mouth lift at the corners before it parted to crush down on hers, just before she closed her eyes, and the doubts and fears and warning signals retreated to some distant corner of her mind and huddled there, ignored.

CHAPTER ELEVEN

SAMANTHA had never been kissed quite like this before, with passion and persuasion and frank enjoyment, yet with a faint edge of something approaching anger. And she had never kissed as she did now, eager and open and revelling in the taste of Jase, the texture of his lips, the brush of his unshaven cheek against her skin.

She thrust her fingers into his hair, loving the silky thickness of it, and when he touched her breast again she arched her back, asking for more even as his mouth opened hers wider, his tongue a welcome invasion. She felt him fumble with the small buttons on her prim cotton blouse, then give up and rip it apart, and his hand was on her bare flesh, shoving aside the lacy edge of her bra to caress and tease.

She moved her own hands across his shoulders, down his chest, and then under his shirt, sliding them over the skin of his back, feeling the firm muscle and bone beneath. Her fingers danced up the groove of his spine, and their kisses became deeper and wilder, until she thought she knew every millimetre of his mouth, and he of hers.

She felt him surge against her groin, and his hands pressed her to him, then he wrenched his mouth from hers, kissed her cheek, her jawbone, her throat, and muttered, "We need to find a bed."

Desperately, her mind agreed. "I know where there is one," she told him, her voice low and throaty.

He grinned, a flash of teeth reminding her she'd once thought he looked like a pirate. His eyes were brilliant with desire, and she knew hers were glazed with it too. "Show me," he said in a guttural growl. But as if he couldn't resist her mouth he kissed her again, accompanied by a slow movement of his pelvis that made her gasp into his mouth.

She pulled away from the kiss. "This way. Don't let me go."

He moved so he was behind her, his arms about her, both hands on her breasts, his mouth dropping kisses on her neck, and they inched towards the bedroom, stopping for more kisses.

On the way she lost her blouse, and once she turned in his arms to shove up his shirt, pulling it off when he raised his arms for her, then he wound them tightly about her and bent her backward to nuzzle at her breasts, the stubble on his cheeks and chin adding an erotic edge she'd never experienced before.

They finally reached her bedroom. As she bent to fold back the cream satin cover he undid the clasp of her bra and the flimsy garment slithered away down her arms.

Still holding her with one arm, he hauled back the bed-clothes with the other and they fell onto the sheet, limbs entwined, mouths and hands searching for each other, shedding their remaining clothing, kissing, touching, exploring. Jase grabbed a packet from his denims and ripped it open, came back to her and looked into her eyes, his own feverish.

"Yes," she said, her body already writhing in anticipation. "Jase…"

He gave her his piratical, feral smile, and poised himself

over her, then plunged deeply, and she opened her mouth in a silent cry of abandon, wound her arms about him, clung, moved beneath him, felt him move in answer, his breath on her cheek, one hand cupped about her breast, his body hers.

He rolled over, bringing her on top of him, sending her into ecstasy such as she'd never known was possible—out of her mind, out of her body, flying weightless into some other cataclysmic dimension.

He bucked beneath her, giving a hoarse cry of satisfaction, and she felt her own pleasure build again and explode dazzlingly, before fading into aftershocks until they both lay still and quiet.

Jase roused himself first, turned over and withdrew, before returning to her and kissing her on the lips, then on her breasts, each one in turn, her belly-button, her thighs.

His hand stroked from her thigh over her hip, rested on her breast, and he kissed her again—softly, sweetly. He retrieved the sheet and settled beside her, his body warm and strong against her. She turned her head to look at him. The room was dim, only a glow from the lamp in the living room allowing them to see each other.

She thought her heart was going to burst right out of her chest, she loved him so much. For the first time in her life she had held nothing back, given him every part of her to do with as he willed. Let her emotions lead her mind.

Did he know that? Had he reciprocated in kind? Or did he always make love like that, wholly absorbed in his partner, knowing intuitively what she wanted from him, leading her to unthought-of heights, giving so generously of himself?

He looked back at her, his eyes shining, even in the near-darkness. "All right, princess?" he asked quietly.

"Yes." *I love you.* She couldn't say it aloud. It would put him under an obligation. He didn't love her and probably never would. It would be stupid to think love had anything to do with this, on his part. Stupid and futile.

She closed her eyes, hoping he didn't see the incipient tears, despising them. She'd gone into this knowingly, prepared for once to take a risk such as she usually only dared take in business. No one had forced her, certainly not Jase. Now she had to live with whatever consequences ensued.

"I knew," he said quietly. "Deep down I always knew. You can't hide from me any more."

His lips touched her temple, then her eyelids one by one. "Sleep, princess," he said, and gathered her closer in his arms.

And, strangely comforted by that, after a few minutes she did.

She woke to sunlight and the sound of the shower in her bathroom. The bedclothes were rumpled, the pillow next to her dented in the middle, and for a few moments she didn't know why she felt so…replete and rested, or why the shower was running.

Then she remembered, and sat bolt upright, grabbing at the sheet as she realised she was naked.

What had she done?

The shower stopped, and she fought the tangled sheet to get out of the bed and find a short satin robe, belting it round her middle. She picked up a brush from the dressing table and swiped it over her hair, the mirror showing flushed cheeks and wild eyes. *Calm down*, she told herself, dropping the brush when she heard the bathroom doorknob turn.

She took a deep breath and slowly turned in time to see Jase appear in the doorway, heartbreakingly, magnificently sexy in only his jeans, zipped but not fastened, the leather belt hanging loose.

"Hi," he said, looking almost as wary as she felt. "Did I wake you? Sorry, but I have to work today."

"So do I." She watched him walk toward her, with the easy, confident and very masculine stride she'd come to love. In fact she loved everything about him.

"You look…different this morning," he said, tipping her face up with his long fingers and regarding her curiously.

"No makeup," she said. It had disappeared during their lovemaking, or else through the night. He'd see how plain she really was.

A smile touched his lips. "It's more than that, beautiful." The word was an endearment, like sweetheart or darling, and her heart turned over. He kissed her lightly, then lingered, his lips tracing the shape of hers. "I have to go," he said gruffly, finally stepping back. "Will you be here if I come back tonight?" His eyes searched hers, as if he might not be sure of the answer.

"Yes." She'd already taken the first, fatal step into the unknown. Too late to go back now.

"We need to talk," he said.

A sliver of fear entered her chest. "Last night you said only one thing mattered."

"Last night—" he gave her a crooked grin "—I was overcome by lust."

Samantha blinked. To Jase a digging implement would always be a spade. She knew that. The only surprise should have been that the words he'd used the previous night to tell her what he wanted to do with her hadn't begun with F.

Come to think of it, she'd never heard him really swear. In

so many ways he had the manners of a true gentleman—the difference between an outward show of etiquette and real consideration and courtesy born of respect.

"You okay?" he asked.

"Yes." Her smile was a little bleak. "I was just thinking of a *Bible* story about the son who said he'd go to the vineyard when his father asked, but didn't, and the one who refused but went anyway." Deeds spoke louder than words. Surely he couldn't have made love to her with such passion and such gentleness, such care for her pleasure, and appreciation of her pleasuring him, if he still despised and mistrusted her. Could he?

He gave her an extremely quizzical, taken-aback look, obviously not understanding the allusion. "Tell me tonight." Then he touched her cheek and walked to the door.

Samantha bought a bouquet of roses, baby's breath and violets from the florist near her office before entering the building, and got Judy to find a vase and place them on her desk, where they scented her day. Several times she caught herself staring at them and thinking of Jase, and checking her watch as the hours crawled by.

Sex, she warned herself, didn't mean Jase would suddenly see her as a maligned innocent. It hadn't solved the problem; more likely it had compounded it.

That didn't stop her longing to see him that night, although uncertain as to what might come of it. When she got home she showered, and ensured her skin all over was smooth and soft before putting one dab of expensive perfume at the hollow of her throat.

She riffled through her wardrobe and chose a simple flowered silk dress she'd hardly worn, having dubbed it a mistake because it was too feminine for business and too casual for formal functions. The lined crossover bodice dipped low in the front—too low for a bra, hence the lining—and the skirt flared at the hem.

After reapplying a discreet amount of makeup, she slid her feet into slipper-style flat shoes, then busied herself opening a bottle of a very good red wine to let it breathe, wondering what time Jase was likely to arrive. She supposed he must be still in Auckland, rather than driving back to Hamilton this morning, though he hadn't said where he had to be and she hadn't thought to ask.

After watching the six o'clock news and an hour of current affairs she made herself a snack and poured a glass of wine that she drank slowly, with a CD of classical favourites playing in the background, and the day's newspaper spread across the kitchen table. She'd read the business section and almost all the news and comment when the doorbell rang. She stood up, smoothed her hair and her dress, and waited for half a minute before walking to the door. The bell rang again before she got there.

Jase was wearing a white self-striped business shirt with dark trousers, but no jacket, and his collar was undone. In one hand he had a fat, long-necked bottle with a gold foil top.

He walked in and surveyed her from top to toe and back again. "I like the dress," he said. "Though I like what's in it even better."

She closed the door behind him, saying dryly, "Do come in!" as he headed for the living room.

He sent her a grin over his shoulder and stepped back to let her go first. Holding out the bottle, he said, "I got this on the way. It's already chilled."

As she took the bottle from him he studied her and said, "And maybe that's not all that's chilled. What's the matter?"

"Nothing."

But as she made to turn from him he caught her wrist and commanded, "Come on, tell me."

Not wanting to start an argument, she looked away.

"What?" he insisted. "You had a bad day? I should have sent flowers? I'm too early?" He looked her over again, and some penny seemed to drop. "Or too late?" Something must have shown in her face because he paused, and then said, "Sorry. I didn't want to take anything for granted—like you giving me dinner. So I figured you'd need time to eat first."

"I did," she said. A few bits of cheese and leftover dip with crackers. "We didn't arrange a time. It's quite all right."

She made to pull away from him, but his grip on her wrist tightened. "Hey," he said, "it's not all right. I'm the guy you slept with last night, and that I hope you're going to sleep with tonight. If you're wild with me, say so. Don't go all gracious lady on me." He tipped his head with a quizzical smile. "*Should* I have brought flowers?"

"I don't think you're the flowers type."

"Uh-huh," he said noncommittally. "What type am I?" His hand slipped from her wrist to close about her fingers.

Not a type at all. He was uniquely Jase, quite unlike any other man she'd known, and certainly not one she'd ever thought she'd fall for, so heavily, so irrevocably. She shook her head. "Indescribable."

"Uh-huh," he said again, his eyes wary and much too inquisitive. "I'm hoping that's a compliment."

She didn't enlighten him, and he dragged her closer,

dropped a kiss on her mouth and said, "If it's any help, I've spent all day counting the minutes."

She didn't say *Me too*. Pulling away from him, she asked, "Do you want to open this?" and led the way across the lounge to the kitchen.

He dealt with the bottle efficiently, but must have noticed the open bottle of red on the counter top. "Would you rather have that?"

"Not now." She set two flutes in front of him. "Are we celebrating?"

"I am." He cocked an inquiring brow at her.

Samantha didn't respond, and he picked up the filled glasses, handed one to her and touched his against it. "To last night," he said. "And many more to come." It didn't sound like a question but she knew it was.

He waited until she'd taken a sip, feeling the bubbles explode in her mouth and tasting the cool crispness of the wine, before he lifted his own glass to his lips. It was the only sign she gave that she had accepted his toast, accepted that they were lovers.

They took the drinks and the bottle into the living room, and he pulled her down beside him onto one of the couches, drawing her close with an arm about her shoulders. Gradually she felt herself relax against him, enjoying the warmth and male muscularity of his body, the slight rise and fall of his breathing, the subtle masculine scent of skin and cotton and a hint of leather.

For a while they sat in silence. The CD she'd put on earlier had automatically restarted, and was playing "None But the Lonely Heart." Years ago in a fit of teenage melancholy she'd decided it was her very own theme song, and even though she'd grown out of feeling sorry for herself the tune still had the power to stir her emotions. She sighed, and Jase said, "What?"

"Nothing."

She took another sip from her glass, and he said, "When are you going to talk to me?"

"You were the one who said you wanted to talk."

"I said *we* need to talk."

Samantha eased out of his hold and reached for the wine bottle, topping up her glass although it was only half empty. "Do we?" She leaned back into the corner of the two-seater and drank some more, then regarded him with deliberate provocation over the rim of the glass. "You weren't so keen last night."

He smiled. "I'm easily distracted. One of the complaints my teachers had." But his eyes were watchful, perhaps even troubled. "I'll have to tell Rachel, you know."

Samantha stiffened. "Tell her what?"

"About you and me…being together."

Samantha's heart plunged. She stood up, uncaring that sparkling wine spilled from her glass onto the carpet.

Tell Rachel? It would be the end of…of any chance to make Jase believe in her, realise how wrong he'd been about the kind of person she was. Maybe even love her.

She put the glass down on the low table. "No!" she said. *"No!"*

She knew she sounded panic-stricken, terrified.

Rachel had done enough damage, wrecked not only her own marriage to Bryn, but what might have been the beginnings of trust between her brother and Samantha. The woman was a loose cannon, and who knew where her next fatal shot would land?

Frowning, Jase put down his glass, his expression intransigent. "She's bound to find out eventually, even way down in Dunedin," he said. "I don't want her hearing it from someone else."

Fear and hope tangled in her breast. He was suggesting their relationship might be long-term, but how long could it last if his sister was determined to break it up? Which surely she would be, in case Jase found out she'd lied to him.

Should she tell him the truth? That the boot—or the stiletto—had been on the other foot, Rachel apparently covering for her own infidelity? But Bryn hadn't told him, and Samantha knew he'd implicitly relied on her silence. Whether he was protecting his faithless wife or his own masculine pride, Samantha couldn't breach his confidence.

"No," she repeated yet again. "No one needs to know about us. At least not yet."

She could see Jase's expression beginning to set. Trepidation made her heart beat harder. Mustering every weapon in her arsenal, leaning towards him, she let her shoes fall to the floor as she tucked her legs behind her. The bodice of her dress gaped, giving him an eyeful of cleavage. Her hand rested on the buttons of his shirt, her mouth inches from his, her eyes pleading. "It can wait," she breathed. "Can't it?" She wasn't, after all, her mother's daughter for nothing.

Her fingers deftly undid a button, then another, and she lowered her head, kissed his bare skin, and smiled to herself as she heard—felt—his indrawn breath.

"Sam," he said. "Samantha—"

He pulled her away, holding her head in his hands, looked at her searchingly, and must have seen the desperation in her eyes. His mouth for a moment went taut, his eyes stormy.

Then his fingers in her hair dragged her up to him, and he kissed her with a kind of wild abandon, his hand delving into the low neckline of her dress, making her pulse roar, her head spin as he caressed her. "No bra," he muttered against her lips, shifting their position so her head rested on the back of the sofa.

She smiled again. "No," she agreed, their lips still touching while his fingers did amazing things to her breasts. "Not with this dress."

He made a small sound like a groan, said, "It's a great dress," and kissed her thoroughly again.

When they came up for air he grumbled, "Why don't you get a decent sofa?" He pulled her up with him and headed for her bedroom.

Her last conscious thought was that she'd at least gained some precious time.

In the weeks following they took unending pleasure in each other's bodies, insatiable for the touch, the taste, the knowledge of each other.

She hadn't known that sex could be both passionate and playful, that delight could be found in a man's fingertip caress or his lightest kiss on any part of her body. That her greatest pleasure would be in seeing him react to her reciprocal stroking and kissing, or that she would dare offer him the most intimate of foreplay and find her own arousal so overwhelming, her climax so completely shattering.

Sometimes they were in her bed five minutes from Jase's arrival; other times they talked for hours, listened to music or watched DVDs while nibbling snacks, Jase's arm about her, his hand on her breast, her head tucked close to his chin. He was the only man she had snuggled up to since as a small child she'd sat on her father's lap. It felt good. Almost wondrous.

He introduced her to more computer games, laughing at her ferocious determination to win, her flushed, crowing pleasure when she did. And she taught him how to do the cryptic cross-words that she wrestled with each weekend, not giving up until she'd solved them. They played strip poker and invented forfeit games that inevitably ended in her bed.

They never discussed his sister, and never went out together. She even refused to visit Jase at his Auckland base, let alone go back to his Waikato home. She knew it frustrated him, but also that as soon as their affair became public he would insist on telling his sister. And if Rachel stuck to her story...

He'd have to make a choice. And Samantha was deathly afraid it wouldn't be her he chose.

She knew he chafed at the restrictions. A secret affair was against his nature. In her more pragmatic moods she told herself this couldn't last anyway, that one day Jase would tire of the situation, the complications—of her—and break it off. On more hopeful days she dreamed about breaking out of the prison of doubt and fear, of seeing Jase stand by her against his sister, his family and the world, declare his faith in her. That he believed her no matter what.

But she didn't dare test it.

One day as she was talking to Bryn at a fundraising dinner they'd attended, he said, in the middle of a discussion on the latest financial crisis, "Has Jase ever said anything about Rachel to you?"

Taken by surprise, she didn't answer immediately. "Why

are you asking me?" she parried, giving herself time to think, a tactic she'd learned to use in business.

"You must have talked sometimes when you were working together on your new systems. Did he mention where she is now?"

"Dunedin," she answered automatically, remembering Jase had mentioned it the night they'd argued about him telling Rachel they were lovers.

"Where in Dunedin?" Bryn demanded, leaning forward across the table where they were having drinks.

Samantha shook her head. "That's all I know. Why?"

He looked down into the whisky glass before him. She saw his fingers curl about it, his knuckles turning white. "I want her back, Sam," he said, his voice low but determined. "I don't care what she's done, or why. She must have had a reason, though I'm damned if I can say I understand, or ever will. All I know is she belongs with me at Rivermeadows."

Struck dumb, she felt first terror, then a fierce, furious wave of jealousy. Why couldn't Jase be like his brother-in-law, who loved his errant wife so much that nothing else mattered, even the ultimate betrayal of adultery?

She wanted that kind of faith from Jase. The kind that went with love. Commitment. Promises and vows.

She could try to dissuade Bryn, remind him of all the reasons Rachel didn't deserve a second chance. But he was her friend, whose pain she'd seen for months, however he tried to hide it. So she sat silent.

"I have to find her," Bryn said, strain in his eyes, his voice. "I have to see her. Her parents say she asked the family not to tell me where she's living."

"Ask Jase," she said.

* * *

Jase had told her he'd be stuck in Hamilton for a week—that he was needed there for a new project his team was working on, especially since he'd been spending less time there recently. "We'll be doing overtime," he said. "All of us."

"I thought," she said, "your whiz-bang technology eliminated the need to be on the spot." Then wondered if she was sounding like her mother, pouting and wheedling to retain her husband's attention when he said he had business to attend to. She shut her mouth.

He was saying, "There's still nothing quite like a round-table, face-to-face discussion, with all the members of the team sparking off each other—or someone calling to someone else across the computer room with a new idea to try, or saying, 'Come and see this,' or 'I need a bit of help here.' That's how we work best."

When he left her he kissed her long and lingeringly, withdrawing with obvious reluctance. "Don't forget me," he said, tweaking her hair. "I'll be back."

He phoned her twice during the week, but they were short, unsatisfactory conversations—no sweet nothings whispered down the line. His forte, she thought with wry amusement, was action rather than words. Maybe that was one reason he'd accepted her embargo on discussing his sister's behaviour.

When he did arrive on her doorstep he carried a bunch of roses—red roses. She wondered if he knew they were supposed to signify love, but perhaps that bit of romantic folklore had passed him by. Extravagantly florist-wrapped in traditional cellophane and coloured paper and tied with a bow, they smelled heavenly too.

He said, "See, I am a flower guy after all when the occasion warrants it." And his kiss was everything a woman might have expected after a week apart. But when the bouquet was crushed between them she made a small protesting sound and eased him away.

"Sorry," he said. "Did you get a thorn?"

"They don't have any," she assured him.

"They don't?"

"Florists' roses are bred without them these days." She fingered a velvety petal, inhaling their perfume. "Sometimes the scent gets bred out too but these are lovely, thank you."

He caught her hand and sniffed at her fingers, then kissed them one by one, taking the last one into his mouth while his eyes teased.

She shuddered all the way to her toes with sheer pleasure, and he lifted his head, his eyes glazed. He said, "I want to take you to bed right now, but I'm trying to be civilized—and anyway, I've got something to tell you. Go and put those things in water or whatever, and maybe I should do the same myself. Only that would mean getting naked, and if I do that…"

She laughed, and left him. It occurred to her she'd never laughed so often as she had, in bed and out of it, since Jase became her lover.

When she came out of the kitchen with the flowers in a vase he was lounging on her new velvet-covered sofa, his feet up, shoes off, and hands behind his head against a plump, soft cushion.

"You bought new furniture," he said.

"Yes." She blushed despite herself. She had seen the sofa—deep and wide and a rich ruby-red, with its own fat, soft matching cushions—in the window of a furniture store, and had immediately fantasised lying on it with Jase, snuggling together, kissing, making love.

She put his flowers down on the low parquet table that she'd decided would complement the sofa better than the previous steel and glass oblong.

"Come here," Jase said, swinging his denim-clad legs down and patting the fabric beside him.

"Don't you want a drink or something?"

"I want you," he said. "Right here with me."

She couldn't help smiling, no doubt a dopey, smitten smile that betrayed everything she felt about him. For once she didn't care, sitting primly beside him on the roomy sofa, laughing when he grabbed her and pulled her to his chest, bringing up his legs again to tangle with hers.

She rested her head on his shoulder, playing with a button on his blue cotton shirt, and said, "What did you want to tell me?"

"Rachel's back."

"Back?" Her hand stilled. She raised her head to look at him, trepidation thrumming inside her.

"With Bryn. They're together again."

CHAPTER TWELVE

"BRYN made me give up her address," Jase said. "We had a...full and frank discussion, as the politicians say."

"He didn't hit you again?" Samantha scanned his face for telltale marks.

"No. It was a near thing. But it wouldn't have worked. I would never have told him except—"

"Except?"

"He loves her. She didn't believe that—and maybe he didn't know himself how much until she left him. She was wrong about everything. So—" he reached up to pull her head down against him again, and kissed her hair "—I told her about us and she's fine with it."

Rachel admitted she was wrong? And magnanimously gave her approval of their relationship?

Samantha shut her eyes, trying to keep a lid on her rising anger, to blot out all but the warmth of him against her cheek, his arm hugging her close, the growing hardness pressing snugly between her thighs, the hot, tingling dampness it aroused.

His arm tightening about her, he lifted her head again, holding it between his hands. His eyes were intent and purposeful. "I love you, Samantha Magnussen. And I want the world to know."

She stared at him in confusion, and he frowned. "Sam?"

It was what she'd wanted, longed for, despaired would never happen. But something cold and ominous was uncurling deep inside her.

He said, "Samantha." And he kissed her, shifting aside so that her back was wedged against the warm velvet, her head pressed into a cushion. Jase's legs wound around hers, the unmistakable erection imprisoned by his jeans pressing at her groin.

The kiss was thorough and persuasive and full of want and need and promise. But the growing, resentful fury inside her turned hot and pulsing and rose to her throat. She didn't kiss him back.

His weight restricted her movements, but she managed to push against him, her hands tight fists, and he drew away, his eyes glazed with passion. "What is it?" he murmured, and kissed her cheek, then shifted his body a little, giving her room. "Am I too heavy?"

"Yes." Pushing his legs out of the way, Samantha stood up, her own legs trembling. She was heated and flushed on the outside, and hurting and furious on the inside. Her head was buzzing and her temples throbbed. She felt she might burst into flames any minute. It was as if another person, an alien presence, had taken over her body. "Too heavy, too *thick* and too sure of yourself!" Her voice didn't sound like her own, high and thin and much too loud. "If you really loved me, you wouldn't have waited until now to tell me!"

"I thought you—"

"Until your *sister* gave you permission!" Still in that alien voice. But she couldn't stop herself—or the shrew who now inhabited her skin.

"That's not how—" Jase began forcefully.

She cut in, "*Now* you believe me?" She had her hands on her hips like the proverbial fishwife, horrifying some small, rational part of her mind. But there was something intensely, dizzyingly liberating about standing over Jase, who seemed glued to the sofa, transfixed, an arrested, oddly calculating expression on his face.

"Did she tell you *why* she lied?" Because there was no excuse that Samantha could think of. Not a viable one. "I must remember to thank her for putting you straight."

"Sam," he said, with irritating patience, which for some reason made her want to kiss him. Or hit him.

"My name's *Samantha*!" she spat, trying to regain her usual sang-froid and treat him with the icy contempt he deserved. Though inside something was splintering apart, maybe her heart. She heard her voice wobble, and—terrified she was about to cry—deliberately whipped up her temper again. "And you can take that holier-than-thou, superior look off your face! *Rachel* might be fine with us, but I'm not! Not if you—"

"Samantha, *listen to me*!" She could see he was holding on to his temper, and that only fuelled hers.

"Why? You didn't listen to me!"

Deaf to everything but her own rage, she stepped back, almost tripping over the forgotten table behind her, she heard the vase of flowers rock and instinctively turned.

Red roses were for love. They blurred before her eyes, that were hot with tears, and without thought she snatched the vase up, whirled and emptied its entire contents over Jase, saying, "And *that* for your damned flowers."

She saw his eyes widen, anger thin his mouth. He'd thrown up his hands automatically in defence but too late—he was soaked all the way to his crotch, one rose lodged in his thick hair, others on his legs and surrounding him on the sofa or the floor, droplets running down the velvet to the carpet.

He let out an explosive word she'd never heard him use before, making her flinch, then his mouth opened and he let out a roar...of laughter.

Still laughing, he lay back on the sofa, dislodging the rose from his hair. Samantha stood over him, totally confounded and indignant, the angry tears drying on her cheeks.

"Don't you laugh at me!" She dropped the vase unheeded to the floor and threw herself at him, pounding on his chest with her fists, not caring that her dress—the dress he'd liked so much—was absorbing water from his clothes, or that despite an "Oomph!" of surprise at her attack and then an "Ow!" a second later he was still laughing while trying to fend her off with raised arms.

She landed a punch in his lower midriff that made him grunt and the laughter stopped, but it remained in his eyes. "Queensbury rules, please," he reproved, still grinning wolfishly. "That one was unladylike. Try aiming for the chin."

The hell with rules, she told him mentally, her eyes delivering the message. She did aim for his face, but he caught her wrist in an iron grip, easily holding her away. "Having fun?" he inquired grimly.

She was on top of him, along the length of his body, and he suddenly parted his thighs, clamping her hips between them. She shifted backward, trying to get a purchase to drive her knee into his groin.

"Oh, no!" he said, and grabbed her other wrist, deftly

turning and letting her fall with a soft thump onto the carpeted floor, following her down. "Not that bit, darling," he chided. "We might need it later." He imprisoned her legs again with his, his hands holding her wrists behind her head.

"Not on your life!" she told him. "You blind, arrogant, conceited jerk!" She tried to head-butt him, but he was prepared for it and dodged, so she only ricked her neck and fell back against the carpet, squashing a rose, its scent rising about her. "And I'm not your darling, damn you!"

"You can do better than that," he goaded. "You must know some proper cuss words."

"I wouldn't stoop so low," she said, trying to rise above her baser instinct to let loose with every swear word she knew. He was taking his weight on his hands although they still held hers, but his pelvis was pressing urgently against her. She heaved her entire body upward, trying to dislodge him, but had no effect at all. "Let me go!" she said, injecting as much fury as she could into the command.

"Uh-uh. You might attack me again."

Much good it had done her. She glared at him. "You can't hold me here all night."

"Mmm." He cocked his head, apparently thinking, a wickedly considering look in his eyes. "I could tie you to the bed. We haven't tried that yet."

"Don't you dare even think about it!"

The picture in her own mind shocked her. Even more shocking was her body's primal reaction to it. Momentarily she closed her eyes, hoping he wouldn't have noticed, then opened them again, to see his expression had changed, and caught her breath.

"Only if you want me to," he said. And kissed her.

It was soft and sweet and tender and…surely loving? She tried to ignore the melting sensation inside her, remained stubbornly unresponsive to the gentle, persuasive movements of his lips, counted to ten, twenty, opened her eyes wide and found her vision filled with Jase's closed lids and his dark, heavy lashes, her nostrils with his aphrodisiac scent, and she closed her eyes again tightly as tears burned her eyes and silently escaped anyway, to trickle down into her hair.

There was nothing she could do to stop them. Jase still held her hands imprisoned in his grasp while his mouth wrought heart-rending magic on hers.

Then his lips wandered to her cheek and he tasted the tears and lifted his head, his eyes shocked and concerned. "Oh, honey, don't!" he said.

He started kissing away the tears that still spilled like a river despite her efforts. "It wasn't the way you think," he said. "I didn't ask and Rachel didn't tell me. She doesn't need to."

She opened her eyes and looked at him through the tears that still came. "You said she admitted—"

"That she was wrong about Bryn, shouldn't have left him. Whatever. That's their business." He kissed her mouth briefly. "You were the one who didn't want Rachel to know about us," he reminded her. "I went along with it against my better judgement because you panicked at the idea." He went back to kissing her cheeks, her earlobe, the line of her chin, wiping tears with his tongue, in between murmuring, "I thought you knew…that night I came to you…I told you it didn't matter, remember? Do you really think…I could have loved you… made love with you all this time…?"

He thought she'd known? She struggled against the hold he still had on her wrists, twitched her head aside from his

wandering mouth and glared up at him. The tears, thank
heaven, finally stopped flowing. "I'm not a mind reader!" she
told him in fury. That was his specialty. And even so he wasn't
infallible. "How was I to know, when you never *said*!"

"Didn't know I needed to." He gazed down at her with a quizzical look. "Any more than I needed to be told you love me."

He knew? "What makes you think—" she started indignantly.

"I've been waiting for you to trust me," he said. "Trust me
enough to know that nothing Rachel or anyone could say
would stop me loving you. Enough to say the words out loud.
You can do it."

She glared at him, her emotions so mixed she felt someone
had picked her up and shaken her until she didn't know which
way was up.

He released her hands to cup her face and she tangled her
fingers into the silky thicket of his hair and stared into his
dark, perceptive eyes, then pulled him to her, kissing him
fiercely, mindlessly, allowing all her love and fury and pain
to tumble out in a maelstrom of unrestrained emotion, until
after his first surprise he kissed her back the way she
wanted—not gently but with an equally ferocious passion
that stopped thought, overwhelmed reason, blotted out everything but the need to have each other *now* with no discussion
and no preliminaries.

She moved one hand to his cheek, caressing the rough
texture she'd come to love, having discovered its potential for
mind-blowing titillation, and with the other guided one of his
hands into the neckline of her dress to her breast, already
peaked and longing for his touch.

He made a sound in his throat and raised his head again.
"Bed," he muttered.

"No." She didn't care that the carpet under her hip was wet, that they were wedged between the sofa and the table, and a rose lay in a hard little lump beneath her.

She tried to bring him back to her, but despite his glittering eyes and harsh breath he stood up, dragging her with him, then lifted her into his arms, ignoring her irritated thump at his shoulder and furious scowl. He carried her through to the bedroom, dumped her on the bed and held her down. "Samantha." His voice was unsteady. "Say it."

She said, "Shut up!" And kissed him again, her arms wound about his neck, her raised knee between his thighs.

He groaned deeply and gave in. When she shoved at his shoulder he turned over, holding her tight, their mouths still fused as she ripped the buttons of his shirt apart and undid his belt while he dealt with the zip of her dress.

Jase tore his mouth away from hers. "Tell me!"

He gasped as she yanked at his shirt and pressed her bare breasts against his chest. Her mouth came to his, hot and inviting, and he let her help him out of his shirt, releasing her mouth again to get rid of her dress while her fingers fumbled with the buckle of his belt.

They stripped each other between kisses, apart for only moments. She reached for him, but despite his obvious, magnificent arousal, he grabbed her wrists again, holding her away, a determined grin on his face. "Say it, Sam," he ordered in a Bogart gravel. "Tell me you love me."

Her bare foot kicked his shin. Her face flushed, her body one burning all-consuming mass of desire, she panted, "You bastard, Jase! *Of course* I love you!" before she climbed on top of him again and slid herself onto him, hot and slick with need.

"So," he said, his smile strained as she felt him swell inside her, "you do know some...real swearwords."

She moved on him, holding herself up, inviting his hands on her breasts, watching his tautened face, his glazed eyes, until his mouth went rigid and he gasped, "Sam—*I can't*..."

She felt him surge, and released her own intense, turbulent orgasm, wave after wave spreading throughout her body, up to the top of her head and down to the tips of her toes, taking her over completely for minutes, aeons, and when Jase turned them so she lay back on the bed, and kissed her temple, her eyelids, her open mouth, she came again and again in his arms, eventually exhausted and limp and damp with sweat, hardly noticing when he left her for a few moments, then returned to hold her against him.

Jase wasn't even sure if she was awake. He felt exhausted himself, and exultant, and filled with tenderness for his difficult, brave, exasperating love.

It had been a spectacular meltdown, and exactly what she needed to let out all those myriad emotions she'd kept locked up for...how many years? One day he'd get her to tell him why.

He'd had a fair idea from the few hints she'd let slip that she'd tried to be the son her father never had, while at the same time she'd wanted to follow her mother's very stereotyped feminine approach to life and relationships, which her father seemed to think was the way a woman should be. With two such contradictory roles to play, she must have been conflicted almost her whole life.

No wonder she'd kept her feelings so carefully within bounds, building herself an icy outward shell to hold them in check.

That was well and truly in smithereens now. For Jase, anyway. She'd never be able to freeze him out again. He smiled with satisfaction, remembering her yelling at him, her gorgeous topaz eyes spitting sparks, her hands clenched on her hips, and then pummelling him. She'd been so magnificently, uncontrollably mad with him while he'd egged her on, elated that at last he was seeing the real Samantha, the gloriously passionate, *feeling* woman he'd known all along was beneath the steely surface.

He couldn't help a quiet, delighted laugh, and she stirred against him, her eyelids flickering. She closed her fingers that lay over his heart and gave him a small, tired, feeble pretend-punch. "You're laughing at me again," she said, with an equally feeble attempt at indignation.

"Yeah," he said, supremely satisfied, his hand caressing her shoulder. "And you're attacking me again."

Her lips curved into a smile, her eyes still closed. "You didn't hit me back."

"Next time," he said, and gently kissed her forehead.

"Won't be one."

"Aw," he said.

She raised her fist again, and he caught it and kissed her knuckles. "Sam?"

"Mmm-hmm."

"You know you've got to marry me."

She smiled against his skin. No bended knee, no humble supplication. *So* Jase. "Is that a proposal?"

"Of course it's—" He tugged at her hair, until he could see her face. His expression was absolutely sober. "*Will* you marry me? I want you right here for the rest of my life."

"Even though I tried to beat you up?" She was embarrassed about that.

"That, or I take out a protection order." He rubbed at a

spot on his chest where she'd hit him earlier, but his eyes laughed at her.

She quelled a spontaneous bubble of answering laughter welling up inside her and made a scornful sound. "You won, anyway."

"Yes, I did," he said. "You're mine, to have and to hold. Luckily I like living dangerously."

She gave him a sceptical look. "Hunched over a computer in your parents' garage?" She hadn't quite forgiven him for that.

"I've never told you," he said with what she could see was completely false modesty, "but I used to skydive as a hobby. And Ben and I climbed a few mountains before he settled into married bliss."

Married bliss. It sounded corny—and wonderful. They'd have things to talk about first—her job, his, where they'd live, whether they wanted children…

Of course Jase would want children. A family like his own. And she… Samantha pictured dark-eyed, mop-haired little boys with dirty knees and mischievous, mini-pirate grins, swarming around her and Jase—children they'd want to be with, who'd be loved and cherished for who they were and who they had the potential to be.

She said, "We'll fight." Jase had an unbendable streak and was hard to move once he'd made up his mind—sometimes too quickly. And she had inherited her father's iron will.

Jase said, "I'm looking forward to it."

"Not physically," she added hastily. "I didn't mean to—"

"Honey, I don't care." He laughed again, deep in his throat. "So long as you let me know how you feel."

Samantha gave a long, contented sigh. She couldn't

promise that thirty years of habit would be smashed to nothing overnight, but she knew with certainty that Jase wouldn't reject her, belittle her opinions, insist she control herself, tell her to remember her manners, or slap her down if she went against his wishes.

He might lose his temper but it would an honest-to-goodness, hot-blooded rage, not cold, contemptuous or bullying, and if she lost hers in return he'd accept her anger and allow her to express it. They'd make up later and laugh at themselves and their petty differences. He'd be as pigheadedly loyal to her as he had been to his sister, because she'd be his family, his wife. His one and only love. As he was hers.

"You are an idiot," she told him with a sort of mournful satisfaction, snuggling again onto his chest, "taking me on." She closed her eyes, sighing again comfortably.

"Hey?" he said, gently tugging at her hair again. "Don't go to sleep yet. You haven't said yes."

She smiled against his skin. "Yes," she murmured. "Oh hell, yes."

And slept.

EPILOGUE

"OH, SAMANTHA!" Rachel Donovan's brown eyes widened in shock. "I'm so sorry!"

Samantha had found herself alone with Rachel after the christening of Bryn and Rachel's new son at Rivermeadows. She'd been using one of the bathrooms when she heard a baby wail and, with the noise of the party going on all around, had wondered if anyone else would notice.

Entering the room where the focus of the celebration had been laid to sleep in his carrycot, Samantha had been debating if she should do something or call his parents, when Rachel entered.

Samantha made to leave, but as Rachel picked up her son she said, "No, stay and keep me company."

The baby in her arms, she propped herself against a pillow on the bed, and Samantha gingerly sat at the end.

After setting the baby to her breast, Rachel said simply and directly, "You don't like me, Samantha, do you?"

Samantha's denial rang hollow. For Jase's sake, since their engagement she'd tried to treat Rachel the same way she did Ben and April, but there was always that insistent *Why?* in the back of her mind.

"You know," Rachel said, "I was jealous of you once."

And I of you. Ready to prevaricate, Samantha paused and said instead, "I don't understand." Surely Rachel hadn't lied to keep her brother away from Samantha? Had she? "Is that why you told Jase you'd seen Bryn and me making love?"

"Told him *what*?" At Rachel's startled reaction the baby stopped sucking and began to cry, until she settled him again. "Why on *earth* would you think I did that?" she asked.

Samantha told her why.

Obviously horrified, Rachel said, "But it wasn't like that— Jase got it all wrong! I saw you in the car park with Bryn, and he kissed you goodbye—on the cheek. I'd just been told I couldn't have a baby—" Ignoring Samantha's surprised look at the contentedly suckling infant she held, she rushed on. "And I'd never really believed Bryn loved me. I couldn't help thinking he should have married someone more suited to him, from the same kind of background, and who could give him children. *That's* what I told Jase—I think." She frowned suddenly. "At least, some of it. I don't remember what I said exactly. I was... I'd been drinking Jase's wine all night." And then, stricken, "Oh, Samantha. I'm so sorry! I'll talk to Jase, I promise!"

"There's no need," Samantha said, after trying to follow all that. "He knows there was some mistake. And I think I understand now."

"You do?" Rachel looked puzzled but anxious. "But I *am* sorry if my drunken ramblings caused a problem."

"It's okay," Samantha assured her, adding dryly, "I have some experience with Jase's wine."

Rachel looked at her, then grinned, for a moment looking amazingly like her brother. "I see!"

Samantha laughed. "Not what you're thinking." But close.

Rachel's eyes danced. "No?" Inviting, *Tell me more?*

Still not quite ready to confide details of her relationship with Jase, Samantha shook her head, but realised she could come to like her sister-in-law-to-be, and laughed for sheer relief.

"You've never had a sister before, have you?" Rachel asked. "I didn't, until April married Ben. It's fun. And now there'll be three of us. We'll outnumber the men in the family."

Sisters? A family? A trifle unsteadily, Samantha said, "I'll look forward to it." There was no reason, she thought almost dizzyingly, why she shouldn't. She blinked. Lately she'd had a disconcerting tendency to tears. Happy ones.

Rachel said, "I can let you in on all Jase's childhood escapades."

Intrigued, Samantha said, "He told me you used to play pirates—and that you were the most bloodthirsty of all."

"Oh, really!" A militant light in her eye, Rachel lowered her voice. "Well, let me tell you that Jase..."

Half an hour later, while a replete young Master Donovan drowsed against his mother's shoulder, a tap on the door was followed by Jase peering round it. "Sorry," he said. "I was looking for Sam."

His glance shifted from one to the other of the two women, sharpening, acute. A rush of relief lightened his spirits.

They were both looking back at him the same way, slightly accusing, but smiling as if they shared a secret.

"Come in," Rachel invited. "We were talking about you."

"No, thanks," he said. "If it's girl-talk, I'll leave you to it."

He shut the door again and heard their joint laughter as he walked away, satisfied. One tiny cloud on his and Samantha's ever-deepening relationship had been blown away. He knew

things had been sorted out and everything was fine in his
world and Samantha's, the world they'd share till the end of
their days.

Just fine.

* * * * *

*Harlequin Intrigue top author Delores Fossen presents
a brand-new series of breathtaking romantic suspense!*
TEXAS MATERNITY: HOSTAGES
*The first installment available May 2010:
THE BABY'S GUARDIAN*

Shaw cursed and hooked his arm around Sabrina.

Despite the urgency that the deadly gunfire created, he tried to be careful with her, and he took the brunt of the fall when he pulled her to the ground. His shoulder hit hard, but he held on tight to his gun so that it wouldn't be jarred from his hand.

Shaw didn't stop there. He crawled over Sabrina, sheltering her pregnant belly with his body, and he came up ready to return fire.

This was obviously a situation he'd wanted to avoid at all cost. He didn't want his baby in the middle of a fight with these armed fugitives, but when they fired that shot, they'd left him no choice. Now, the trick was to get Sabrina safely out of there.

"Get down," someone on the SWAT team yelled from the roof of the adjacent building.

Shaw did. He dropped lower, covering Sabrina as best he could.

There was another shot, but this one came from a rifleman on the SWAT team. Shaw didn't look up, but he heard the sound of glass being blown apart.

The shots continued, all coming from his men, which meant it might be time to try to get Sabrina to better cover. Shaw glanced at the front of the building.

So that Sabrina's pregnant belly wouldn't be smashed

against the ground, Shaw eased off her and moved her to a sitting position so that her back was against the brick wall. They were close. Too close. And face-to-face.

He found himself staring right into those sea-green eyes.

How will Shaw get Sabrina out?
Follow the daring rescue and the heartbreaking
aftermath in THE BABY'S GUARDIAN by Delores Fossen,
available May 2010 from Harlequin Intrigue.

Copyright © 2010 by Delores Fossen

Bestselling Harlequin Presents® author

Lynne Graham

introduces

VIRGIN ON HER WEDDING NIGHT

Valente Lorenzatto never forgave Caroline Hales's
abandonment of him at the altar. But now he's
made millions and claimed his aristocratic Venetian
birthright—and he's poised to get his revenge.
He'll ruin Caroline's family by buying out their
company and throwing them out of their mansion…
unless she agrees to give him the wedding night
she denied him five years ago.…

**Available May 2010
from Harlequin Presents!**

www.eHarlequin.com

HP12915

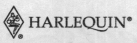

HARLEQUIN®

LAURA MARIE ALTOM

The Baby Twins

Stephanie Olmstead has her hands full raising
her twin baby girls on her own. When she runs
into old friend Brady Flynn, she's shocked to find
herself suddenly attracted to the handsome airline
pilot! Will this flyboy be the perfect daddy—
or will he crash and burn?

Babies
&
Bachelors
USA

"LOVE, HOME & HAPPINESS"

www.eHarlequin.com

HAR75309

HARLEQUIN® *Blaze*™

is proud to present

New York Times bestselling author

Vicki Lewis Thompson

**with a brand-new trilogy,
SONS OF CHANCE
where three sexy brothers
meet three irresistible women.**

Look for the first book

WANTED!

*Available beginning in June 2010
wherever books are sold.*

---

red-hot reads

www.eHarlequin.com

HB79548

LARGER-PRINT BOOKS!

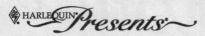 HARLEQUIN *Presents*~

PASSION GUARANTEED SEDUCTION

GET 2 FREE LARGER-PRINT NOVELS PLUS 2 FREE GIFTS!

YES! Please send me 2 FREE LARGER-PRINT Harlequin Presents® novels and my 2 FREE gifts (gifts are worth about $10). After receiving them, if I don't wish to receive any more books, I can return the shipping statement marked "cancel". If I don't cancel, I will receive 6 brand-new novels every month and be billed just $4.55 per book in the U.S. or $5.24 per book in Canada. That's a saving of at least 13% off the cover price! It's quite a bargain! Shipping and handling is just 50¢ per book.* I understand that accepting the 2 free books and gifts places me under no obligation to buy anything. I can always return a shipment and cancel at any time. Even if I never buy another book, the two free books and gifts are mine to keep forever.

176/376 HDN E5NG

Name _____ (PLEASE PRINT)

Address _____ Apt. #

City _____ State/Prov. _____ Zip/Postal Code

Signature (if under 18, a parent or guardian must sign)

Mail to the **Harlequin Reader Service:**
IN U.S.A.: P.O. Box 1867, Buffalo, NY 14240-1867
IN CANADA: P.O. Box 609, Fort Erie, Ontario L2A 5X3

Not valid for current subscribers to Harlequin Presents Larger-Print books.

**Are you a subscriber to Harlequin Presents books
and want to receive the larger-print edition?
Call 1-800-873-8635 today!**

* Terms and prices subject to change without notice. Prices do not include applicable taxes. Sales tax applicable in N.Y. Canadian residents will be charged applicable provincial taxes and GST. Offer not valid in Quebec. This offer is limited to one order per household. All orders subject to approval. Credit or debit balances in a customer's account(s) may be offset by any other outstanding balance owed by or to the customer. Please allow 4 to 6 weeks for delivery. Offer available while quantities last.

Your Privacy: Harlequin Books is committed to protecting your privacy. Our Privacy Policy is available online at www.eHarlequin.com or upon request from the Reader Service. From time to time we make our lists of customers available to reputable third parties who may have a product or service of interest to you. If you would prefer we not share your name and address, please check here. ☐

Help us get it right—We strive for accurate, respectful and relevant communications. To clarify or modify your communication preferences, visit us at www.ReaderService.com/consumerchoice.

HPLP10R

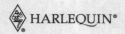

HARLEQUIN®

Showcase

On sale May 11, 2010

Reader favorites from the most talented voices in romance

Save $1.00 on the purchase of 1 or more Harlequin® Showcase books.

SAVE $1.00 on the purchase of 1 or more Harlequin® Showcase books.

Coupon expires Oct 31, 2010. Redeemable at participating retail outlets.
Limit one coupon per purchase. Valid in the U.S.A. and Canada only.

52609015

5 65373 00076 2   (8100)0 11651

Canadian Retailers: Harlequin Enterprises Limited will pay the face value of this coupon plus 10.25¢ if submitted by customer for this product only. Any other use constitutes fraud. Coupon is nonassignable. Void if taxed, prohibited or restricted by law. Consumer must pay any government taxes. Void if copied. Nielsen Clearing House ("NCH") customers submit coupons and proof of sales to Harlequin Enterprises Limited, P.O. Box 3000, Saint John, NB E2L 4L3, Canada. Non-NCH retailer—for reimbursement submit coupons and proof of sales directly to Harlequin Enterprises Limited, Retail Marketing Department, 225 Duncan Mill Rd., Don Mills, ON M3B 3K9, Canada.

U.S. Retailers: Harlequin Enterprises Limited will pay the face value of this coupon plus 8¢ if submitted by customer for this product only. Any other use constitutes fraud. Coupon is nonassignable. Void if taxed, prohibited or restricted by law. Consumer must pay any government taxes. Void if copied. For reimbursement submit coupons and proof of sales directly to Harlequin Enterprises Limited, P.O. Box 880478, El Paso, TX 88588-0478, U.S.A. Cash value 1/100 cents.

® and TM are trademarks owned and used by the trademark owner and/or its licensee.
© 2009 Harlequin Enterprises Limited

HSCCOUP0410

Coming Next Month

in **Harlequin Presents®**. Available April 27, 2010:

#2915 VIRGIN ON HER WEDDING NIGHT
Lynne Graham

#2916 TAMED: THE BARBARIAN KING
Jennie Lucas
Dark-Hearted Desert Men

#2917 BLACKWOLF'S REDEMPTION
Sandra Marton
Men Without Mercy

#2918 THE PRINCE'S CHAMBERMAID
Sharon Kendrick
At His Service

#2919 MISTRESS: PREGNANT BY THE SPANISH BILLIONAIRE
Kim Lawrence

#2920 RUTHLESS RUSSIAN, LOST INNOCENCE
Chantelle Shaw

Coming Next Month

in **Harlequin Presents® EXTRA**. Available May 11, 2010.

#101 THE COSTANZO BABY SECRET
Catherine Spencer
Claiming His Love-Child

#102 HER SECRET, HIS LOVE-CHILD
Tina Duncan
Claiming His Love-Child

#103 HOT BOSS, BOARDROOM MISTRESS
Natalie Anderson
Strictly Business

#104 GOOD GIRL OR GOLD-DIGGER?
Kate Hardy
Strictly Business

HPECNMBPA0410